Charles Monroe Sheldon

The Crucifixion of Phillip Strong

Charles Monroe Sheldon

The Crucifixion of Phillip Strong

ISBN/EAN: 9783337385729

Printed in Europe, USA, Canada, Australia, Japan

Cover: Foto ©Andreas Hilbeck / pixelio.de

More available books at **www.hansebooks.com**

THE CRUCIFIXION

OF

PHILLIP STRONG

BY

CHARLES M. SHELDON

AUTHOR OF

"IN HIS STEPS (WHAT WOULD JESUS DO?),"
"HIS BROTHER'S KEEPER," ETC.

———

CHICAGO
ADVANCE PUBLISHING Co.
215 Madison Street
1898

To the members of Central Church, Topeka, Kansas, and to other friends who listened to the story of Phillip Strong during the winter of 1893, this volume is affectionately dedicated by the author.

INTRODUCTION

To "The Crucifixion of Phillip Strong."

There are men who in the pulpit project and glorify ideals whose dreams of the nobler life melt into fine mist and disappear because no force of purpose put them into action. Preachers often see visions in the Study and display them in the Sanctuary, that nobody else ever sees except in their sermons. The power to idealize and to awaken ideals in others is the first movement towards high art in living as in painting, in building a character as in building a cathedral. But it is only the first movement, and without sequel of resolve and service it is valueless. "Our grand business undoubtedly is," says Thomas Carlyle, "not to see what lies dimly at a distance, but to do what lies clearly at hand." And it is also undoubtedly true that as one does what he sees "clearly at hand" the distant visions lose their dimness and vagueness, and become a part of the immediate horizon. He that "doeth" shall "know." He that "walketh uprightly" and who "shutteth his eyes from seeing evil" will soon "see the King in his beauty and behold the land that is very far off." Dreaming must be transmuted into doing.

The demand of the pulpit in our age is the power to set forth by words well-chosen and by attractive parables which give truth in concrete form, the possibilities of individual and social life. But well-chosen words and illuminating parables must find a still more concrete interpretation in the quality and the deed of the preacher and of the people—the church which he represents.

When I read "The Crucifixion of Phillip Strong" in its first edition I scarcely knew the author; but I felt that a dreamer had seen more than a shadow, and I wondered of what stuff he himself was made. The story, it seemed to me, was born in a soul impressed with, and sometimes oppressed by the reality of life. The earnestness of a divine conviction seemed to run like a fire along every line. I at once wrote to the author concerning the book: "It is a wonderfuly strong and effective contribution to the Christian literature of this age. Every minister ought to read it—and everybody else." The story is "a dream that is not all a dream."

A later and almost intimate acquaintance with my fellow-townsman has confirmed my interpretation of the author of "Phillip Strong." His personal efforts to find out "what Jesus would do if He lived in our age"; his fidelity as a pastor, a preacher and a reformer; his activity and aggressiveness on week-days as on Sundays; his wise and winning way of preaching the ·gospel through his stories, which he reads by chapters as sermons to his Sunday evening congregations; his kindergarten work in his own church, and in another part of town among the little negroes; the impression made by his own spiritual and earnest personality—all prepare me to read what he writes with the conviction ever present that the hand that writes these things is moved by a heart to whom these things are living verities. And I find it easy to say as Dr. Wilkinson in his "Epic of Paul," makes Rachel, Paul's sister, say:

> "O, brother, when such things thou sayest,
> I tremble with unspeakable desire
> To be what thou must be to think such things."

BISHOP JOHN H. VINCENT.

Episcopal Residence, Topeka, Kansas, February 1898.

THE CRUCIFIXION

OF

PHILLIP STRONG.

———•———

CHAPTER I.

PHILLIP STRONG could not decide what it was best to do.

The postman that evening had brought him two letters and he had just finished reading them. He sat with his hands clasped over his knee, leaning back in his chair and looking out through his study window. He was evidently thinking very hard and the two letters were the cause of his perplexity.

Finally he rose, went to his study door and called down the stairs, " Sarah, I wish you would come up here. I want your help."

" All right, Phillip, I 'll be up in a minute," responded a voice from below, and very soon the minister's wife came up-stairs into her husband's study.

" What 's the matter, Phillip ? " she said, as she came into the room. " It must be something very serious, for you don't call me up here unless you are in great distress. You remember the last time you called me, you had shut the tassel of your dressing-gown under the lid of your writing desk and I had to cut you loose. You are n't fast anywhere now, are you?"

Phillip smiled quaintly. "Yes, I am. I'm in a strait betwixt two. Let me read these letters and you will see." So he began at once, and we will copy the letters, omitting dates.

MILTON, CALVARY CHURCH.

REV. PHILLIP STRONG.

DEAR SIR, — At a meeting of the Milton Calvary Church held last week, it was voted unanimously to extend to you a call to become pastor of this church at a salary of two thousand dollars a year. We trust that you will find it in accordance with the will of the Head of the Church that you accept this decision on the part of Calvary Church and become its pastor. The church is in good condition and has the hearty support of most of the leading families in the town. Both in membership and financially it is the strongest of the principal churches here. We wait your reply, confidently hoping you will decide to come to us. We have been without a settled pastor now for nearly a year, since the death of Dr. B., and we have united upon you as the person most eminently fitted to fill the pulpit of Calvary Church. The grace of our Lord be with you. In behalf of the Church, '

WILLIAM WINTER,
Chairman of the Board of Trustees.

"What do you think of that, Sarah?" asked Phillip Strong, as he finished the letter.

" Two thousand dollars is twice as much as you are getting now, Phillip."

" What, you mercenary little creature, do you think of the salary first ? "

" If I did not think of it once in a while, I doubt if you would have a decent meal or a good suit of clothes," replied the minister's wife, looking at him with a smile.

" Oh, well, that may be, Sarah. But let me read the other letter." He went on without discussing the salary matter.

ELMDALE, CHAPEL HILL CHURCH.

REV. PHILLIP STRONG,

DEAR BROTHER, — At a meeting of the Elmdale Chapel Hill Church held last week Thursday it was unanimously voted to extend you a call to become pastor of the church at a salary of two thousand dollars a year, with two months' vacation, to be selected at your own convenience. The Chapel Hill Church is in a prosperous condition, and many of the members recall your career in our college with much pleasure. This is an especially strong centre for church work, the proximity of the boys' Academy and the University making the situation one of great power to a man who thoroughly understands and enjoys young men as we know you do. We most earnestly hope you will consider this call, not as purely formal, but as from the hearts of the people. We are, very cordially yours,

In behalf of the Church,

PROFESSOR WELLMAN,
Chairman of the Board of Trustees.

" The salary is just the same, is n't it ? " said the minister's wife.

"Now, Sarah," said the minister, "if I did n't know what a generous unselfish heart you really have, I should get vexed at you for talking about the salary as if that were the most important thing."

"The salary is very important, though. But you know, Phillip, I would be as willing as you are to live on no salary if the grocer and butcher would continue to feed us for nothing. I wish from the bottom of my heart that we could live without money."

"It is a bother, is n't it?" replied Phillip, so gravely that his wife laughed heartily at his tone.

"Which of the two churches do you prefer?" asked his wife.

"I would rather go to the Chapel Hill Church as far as my preference is concerned."

"Then why not accept their call if that is the way you feel?"

"Because while I should like to go to Elmdale I feel as if I ought to go to Milton."

"Now, Phillip, I don't see why in a choice of this kind you don't do as you feel inclined to do, and accept the call that pleases you most. Why should ministers always be doing what they ought instead of what they like? You never please yourself."

"Well, Sarah," replied Phillip, good-naturedly, "this is the way of it. The church in Elmdale is in a University town. The atmosphere of the place is scholastic. You know I passed four years of student life there. With the exception of the schools, there are not a thousand people in the village, a quiet, sleepy, dull, retired, studious place. I love the memory of it. I could go there as the pastor of the Elmdale church and preach to an audience of college boys eight months in the year and to about eighty refined, scholarly, Christian people the rest of the time. I could indulge my taste for reading and writing and enjoy a quiet pastorate there to the end of my life."

" Then, Phillip, I don't see why you don't reply to their call and tell them you will accept ; and we will move at once to Elmdale, and live and die there. It is a beautiful place and I am sure we could live very comfortably on the salary and the vacation. There is no vacation mentioned in the other call."

" But, on the other hand," continued the minister, almost as if he were alone and arguing with himself, and had not heard his wife's words, " on the other hand, there is Milton, a manufacturing town of eighty thousand people, most of them connected with the mills. It is the centre of much that belongs to the stirring life of the times in which we live. The labor question is there in the lives of those operatives. There are very many churches of different denominations, to the best of my knowledge, all striving after popularity and power. There is much hard, stern work to be done in Milton by the true Church of Christ to apply his teachings to men's needs, and somehow I cannot help hearing a voice,

' Phillip Strong, go to Milton and work for Christ. Abandon your dream of a parish where you may indulge your love of scholarship in the quiet atmosphere of a University town, and plunge into the hard, disagreeable, but necessary work of this age, in the atmosphere of physical labor, where great questions are being discussed, and the masses are engrossed in the terrible struggle for liberty and home, where physical life thrusts itself out into society, trampling down the spiritual and intellectual, and demanding of the Church and the preacher the fighting powers of giants of God to restore in men's souls a more just proportion of the value of the life of man on the earth.'

"So you see, Sarah," the minister went on after a little pause, " I want to go to Elmdale, but the Lord probably wants me to go to Milton."

Mrs. Strong was silent. She had the utmost faith in her husband that he would do exactly what he knew he ought to do when once he decided what it was. Phillip Strong was also silent a moment. At last he said, " Don't you think so, Sarah? "

" I don't see how we can always tell exactly what the Lord wants us to do. How can you tell that he doesn't want you to go to Elmdale and become pastor of that church ? "

" No doubt there is a necessary work to be done there. The only question is, am I the one to do it or is the call to Milton more imperative? The more I think of it, the more I am convinced that I must go to Milton."

" Then," said the minister's wife, rising suddenly
and speaking with a mock seriousness that her husband fully understood, " I don't see why you called
me up here to decide what you had evidently settled
already. Do you consider that fair treatment, sir?
It will serve you right if those biscuits I put in the
oven when you called me, are fallen as completely
as Babylon. And I will make you eat half a dozen
of them, sir, to punish you. We cannot afford to
waste anything these times."

" What," cried Philip, slyly, " not on two thousand dollars a year! But I'll eat the biscuits.
They can't possibly be any worse than those we had
a week after we were married, — the ones we bought
from the bakery, you remember," Phillip added,
hastily.

" You saved yourself just in time, then," replied
the minister's wife. She came close up to the desk
and in a different tone said, " Phillip, you know I
believe in you, don't you?"

" Yes," said Phillip simply : " I am sure you do.
I am impulsive and impractical, but heart and soul,
and body and mind, I simply want to do the will of
God. Is it not so?"

" I know it is," she said, " and if you go to Milton
it will be because you want to do his will more than
to please yourself."

" Yes. Then shall I answer the letter to-night?"

" Yes, if you have decided, with my help, of
course."

" Of course, you foolish creature, you know I

could not settle it without you. And as for the biscuits — "

"As for the biscuits," said the minister's wife, " they will be settled without me too if I don't go down and see to them." She hurried downstairs and Phillip Strong with a smile and a sigh took up his pen and wrote replies to the two calls he had received, refusing the call to Elmdale and accepting the one to Milton. And so the strange story of a great hearted man really began.

When he had finished writing these two letters he wrote another, which throws so much light on his character and his purpose in going to Milton that we will insert it into this story. This is the letter : —

My dear Alfred, — Two years ago when we left the Seminary you remember we promised each other in case either of us left his present parish he would let the other know at once. I did not suppose when I came here that I should leave so soon, but I have just written a letter which means the beginning of a new life to me. The Calvary Church in Milton has given me a call, and I have accepted it. Two months ago my church here practically went out of existence through a union with the other church on the street. The history of that movement is too long for me to relate here, but since it took place I have been preaching as a supply, pending the final settlement of affairs, and so I was at liberty to accept a call elsewhere. I must confess the call from Milton was a surprise to me. I have never been there (you know I do not believe in candidating for a place), and so I suppose their church committee came up here to listen to me. Two years ago nothing would have induced me to go to Milton. To-day it seems perfectly clear that the Lord says to me " Go." You know my natural inclination is towards a quiet scholarly pastorate. Well, Milton is, as you know, a noisy, dirty manufacturing town full of working men, cursed with saloons, and black with coal smoke and unwashed humanity. The church is quite strong in membership. The Year Book gives it five hundred members last year, and it is composed almost entirely of the leading families in the place. What I can do in such a church remains to be seen. My predecessor there, Dr. B., was a profound sermonizer, and generally liked, I believe. He was a man of the old school and made no attempt, I understand, to bring the church into contact with the masses. You will say that such a church is a poor place in which to attempt a different work. I do not think it is necessarily so. The Church of Christ is in itself, I believe, a powerful engine to set in motion against all evil. I have great faith in the membership of almost any church in this country to accomplish wonderful things for humanity. And I am going to Milton with that faith very strong in me. I feel as if a very great work could be done there. Think of it, Alfred! A town of eighty thousand working-people, half of them foreigners, a town with more than one hundred saloons in full blast, a town with many churches of many different denominations, the seven largest situated on one street, and that street the most fashionable one in the place, a town where the police records show an amount of crime and depravity almost unparalleled in Municipal annals, — surely such a place presents an opportunity for the true Church of Christ to do some splendid work. I hope I do not over-estimate the needs of the place. I have known the general condition of things in Milton ever since you and I did our summer work in the neighboring town of Clifton. If ever there was missionary ground in America it is there. I cannot understand just why the call comes to me to go to a place and take up work that in many ways is so distasteful to me. In one sense I shrink from it with a sensitiveness which no one except my wife and you could understand. You know what an almost ridiculous excess of sensibility I have. It seems sometimes impossible for me to do the work that the active ministry of this age demands of a man. It almost kills me to know that I am criticised for all I say and do. And yet I know that the ministry will always be the target for criticism. I have an almost morbid shrinking from the thought that people do not like me, that I am not loved by everybody, and yet I know that if I speak the truth in my preaching and speak it without regard to consequences, some one is sure to become offended, and in the end dislike me. I think the good God never made a man with so intense a craving for the love of his fellow-men as I possess. And yet I am conscious that I cannot make myself understood by very many people. They will always say, " How cold and unapproachable he is." When in reality I love them with yearning of the heart after them. Now, then, I am going to Milton with all this complex thought of myself, and yet, dear chum, there is not the least doubt after all that I ought to go. I hope that in the rush of the work there I shall be able to forget myself. And then the work will stand out prominent as it ought. With all my doubts of myself I never question the wisdom of entering the ministry. I have a very positive assurance as I work that I am doing what I ought to do. And what can a man do more? I am not dissatisfied with the ministry, only with my own action within it. It is the noblest of all professions ; I feel proud of it every day. Only, it is so great that it makes a man feel small when he steps inside.

Well, my wife is calling me down to tea. Let me know what you do. We shall move to Milton next week, probably, so, if you write, direct there. As ever, your old chum,

PHILLIP STRONG.

It was characteristic of Phillip that in this letter he said nothing about his call to Elmdale, and did not tell his college chum what salary was offered him by the church at Milton. As a matter of fact he really forgot all about everything except the one important event of his decision to go to Milton. He regarded it, and rightly, as the most serious step of his life ; and while he had apparently decided the matter very quickly, his decision was, in reality, the result of a deep conviction that he ought to go. He was in the habit of making his decisions rapidly. This habit sometimes led him into embarrassing mistakes, and once in a great while resulted in humiliating reversals of opinion, so that people who did not know him thought he was irresolute and fickle. In the present case Phillip acted with his customary quickness, and knew very well that his action was unalterable.

Within a week he had moved to Milton, as the church wished him to occupy the pulpit at once. The parsonage was a well-planned house next the church, and his wife soon made everything very homelike. The first Sunday evening after Phillip preached at Milton for the first time, he chatted with his wife over the events of the day as they sat before a cheerful open fire in the large grate. It was late in the fall and the nights were sharp and frosty.

" Are you tired to night, Phillip? " asked his wife.

" Yes, the day has been rather tiring. Did you think I was nervous? Did I preach as well as usual? " Phillip was not vain in the least. He simply put the question to satisfy his own exacting demand upon himself in preaching. And there was not a person in the world to whom he would have put such a question except his wife.

" No, I thought you did splendidly. I felt proud of you. You made some queer gestures, and once you put one of your hands in your pocket. But your sermons were both strong and effective; I am sure the people were impressed. It was very still at both services."

Phillip was silent a moment. And his wife went on.

" I am sure we shall like this place, Phillip; what do you think? "

" I cannot tell yet. There is very much to do."

" How do you like the church building? "

" It is an easy audience room for my voice. I don't like the arrangement of the choir over the front door. I think the choir ought to be down on the platform in front of the people by the side of the minister."

" That 's one of your hobbies, Phillip. But the singing was good, did n't you think so? "

" Yes, the choir is a good one. The congregation does n't seem to sing much, and I believe in Congregational singing even where there is a choir. But we can bring that about in time, I think."

"Now, Phillip," said his wife, in some alarm, "you are not going to meddle with the singing, are you? You will get into trouble. There is a musical committee in the church, and such committees are very sensitive about any interference."

"Well," said Phillip, rousing up a little, "the singing is a very important part of the religious service. And it seems to me I ought to have something important to say about it. But you need not fear, Sarah. I 'm not going to try to change everything all at once."

His wife looked at him a little anxiously. She had perfect faith in Phillip's honesty of purpose but she sometimes had a fear of his impetuous desire to reform the world. After a little pause she spoke again, changing the subject.

"What did you think of the congregation, Phillip?"

"I enjoyed it. I thought it was very attentive. There was a larger number out this evening than I had expected."

"Did you like the looks of the people?"

"They were all very nicely dressed."

"Now, Phillip, you know that is n't what I mean. Did you like the people's faces?"

"You know I like all sorts and conditions of men."

"Yes, but there are audiences, and audiences. Do you think you will enjoy preaching to this one in Calvary Church?"

"I think I shall," replied Phillip, but he said it in a tone that might have meant a great deal more. Again there was silence, and again the minister's wife was the first to break it.

"There was a place in your sermon to-night, Phillip, where you appeared the least bit embarrassed; as you seem sometimes at home when you have some writing or some newspaper article on your mind and some one suddenly interrupts you with a question far from your thoughts. What was the matter? Did you forget a point?"

"No, I'll tell you. From where I stand on the pulpit platform I can see through one of the windows over the front door. There is a large electric lamp burning outside, and the light fell directly on the sidewalk, across the street. From time to time groups of people went through that band of light. Of course I could not see their faces very well, but I soon found out that they were mostly the young men and women operatives of the mills. They were out strolling through the street, which I am told is a favorite promenade with them. I should think as many as two hundred passed by the church while I was preaching. Well, after awhile I began to ask myself whether there was any possible way of getting those young people to come into the church, instead of strolling past? And then I thought of the people in front of me, and saw how different they were from those outside, and wondered if it would n't be better to close up the church and go and preach on the street where the people were. And this carrying on of all that questioning with myself, while I tried to preach, caused a little 'embarrassment', as you kindly call it, in the sermon."

"I should think so! But how do you know, Phillip, that those people outside were in any need of your preaching?"

Phillip appeared surprised at the question. He looked at his wife, and her face was serious.

"Why, do not all people need preaching? They may not stand in need of *my* preaching, perhaps, but they ought to have some. And I cannot help thinking of what is the duty of the church in this place, to the great crowd outside. Something ought to be done, I know. And something will be done by Calvary Church, in time. I foresee the need of an immense amount of prayer and work. And I need very much wisdom."

"Phillip, I am sure your work will be blessed, don't you think so?"

"I know it will," replied Phillip, with the calm assurance of a very positive, but spiritually minded man. He never thought his Master was honored by being asked for small things, or by men doubting the power of Christianity to do great things.

Always when he said "I" he simply meant, not Phillip Strong, but Christ in Phillip Strong. To deny the power and worth of that incarnation was, to his mind, not humility but treason.

The Sunday following, Phillip made this announcement to his people : —

"Beginning with next Sunday morning I shall

give the first of a series of monthly talks on Christ and Modern Society. It will be my object in these talks to suppose Christ himself as the one speaking to modern society on its sins, its needs its opportunities, its responsibilities, its every-day life. I shall try to be entirely loving and just and courageous in giving what I believe Christ himself would give you if he were the pastor of Calvary Church in Milton to-day. So, during, these talks, I wish you would, with me, try to see if you think Christ would actually say what I shall say in his place. Or, rather, what he would say in my place. If Christ were in Milton to-day, I believe he would speak very plainly, and in many cases he might seem to be severe. But it would be for our good. Of course I am but human in my weakness. I shall make mistakes. I shall probably say things Christ would not say. But always going to the source of all true help, the Spirit of Truth, I shall, as best a man may, speak as I truly believe Christ would if he were your pastor. These talks will be given on the first Sunday of every month. I cannot announce the subjects, for they will be chosen as the opportunities arise."

During the week, Phillip spent several hours of each day in learning the facts concerning the town. One of the first things he did was to buy an accurate map of the place. He hung it up on the wall of his study, and in after days found occasion to make good use of it. He spent his afternoons walking over the town. He noted with special interest and earnestness the great brick mills by the river, five enormous structures with immense chimneys out of which poured great volumes of smoke. Something about the mills fascinated him. They seemed like monsters of some sort, grim, unfeeling, but terrible. As one walked by them he seemed to feel the throbbing of the hearts of five living creatures. The unpainted tenements, ugly in their unfailing similarity, affected Phillip with a sense of something like anger. He had a keen and truthful taste in matters of architecture, and those boxes of houses offended every artistic and homelike feeling in him. Coming home one day past the tenements he found himself in an unknown street, and for the curiosity of it he counted the saloons on the street in one block. There were over twelve. There was a policeman on the corner as Phillip reached the crossing, and he inquired of the officer if he could tell him who owned the property in the block containing the saloons.

" I believe most of the houses belong to Mr. Winter, sir."

" Mr. William Winter?" asked Phillip.

" Yes, I think that's his name. He is the largest owner in the Ocean Mill yonder."

Phillip thanked the man and went on towards home. "William Winter!" he exclaimed. "Is it possible that man will accept a revenue from the renting of his property to these vestibules of hell? That man! One of the leading members in my church! Chairman of the board of trustees and a leading citizen of the place! It does not seem possible!"

But before the week was out Phillip had found out facts that made his heart burn with shame and roused his indignation. Property in the town which was being used for saloons, gambling-houses, and dens of wickedness, was owned in large part by several of the most prominent members of his church. There was no doubt of the fact. Phillip, whose very nature was frankness itself, resolved to go to these men and have a plain talk with them about it. It seemed to him like a monstrously evil thing that a Christian believer, a church-member, should be renting his property to these dens of vice, and taking the money. He called on Mr. Winter; but he was out of town and would not be back until Saturday night. He went to see another member who was a large shareholder in one of the mills, and a heavy property owner. It was not a pleasant thing to do, but Phillip boldly stated the precise reason for his call, and asked if it was true that he rented several houses in a certain block where saloons and gambling-houses were numerous. The man looked at Phillip, turned red, and finally said it was a fact, but none of Phillip's business.

" My dear brother," said Phillip, with a sad but kindly smile, " you cannot imagine what it costs me to come to you about this matter. In one sense, it may seem to you like an impertinent meddling in your business. In another sense, it is only what I ought to do as pastor of a church which is dearer to me than my life. And I have come to you as a brother in Christ to ask if it seems to you like a

thing which Christ would approve that you, his disciple, should allow the property which has come into
your hands that you may use it for his glory and the
building up of his kingdom, to be used by the
agents of the devil while you reap the financial benefit. Is it right, my brother?"

The man to whom the question was put made the
usual excuses, that if he did not rent to these people,
other men would, that there was no call for the property for other purposes, and if it were not rented to
objectionable people it would lie empty at a dead
loss, and so forth. To all of which Phillip opposed
the plain will of God, that all a man has should be
used in clean and honest ways, and He could never
sanction the getting of money through such immoral
channels. The man was finally induced to acknowledge that it was not just the right thing to do, and
especially for a church-member. But, when Phillip
pressed him to give up the whole iniquitous revenue,
and clear himself of all connection with it, the property owner looked aghast.

"Why, Mr. Strong, do you know what you ask?
Two-thirds of the most regular part of my income
is derived from these rents. It is out of the question for me to give them up. You are too nice in
the matter. All the property owners in Milton do
the same thing. There isn't a man of any means
in the church who isn't deriving some revenue from
this source. Why, a large part of your salary is
paid from these very rents. You will get into
trouble if you try to meddle in this matter. I don't

take offence. I think you have done your duty.
And I confess it does n't seem exactly the thing.
But, as society is organized, I don't see that we can
change the matter. Better not try to do anything
about it, Mr. Strong. The church likes you, and it
will support you handsomely; but men are very
touchy when their private business is meddled
with."

Phillip sat listening to this speech, and his face
grew white, and he clenched his hands tighter as the
man went on. When he had finished, Phillip spoke
in a low voice :—

" Mr. Bentley, you do not know me, if you think
any fear of the consequences will prevent my speaking to the members of my church on any matter
where it seems to me I ought to speak. In this
particular matter, I believe it is not only my right,
but my duty to speak. I should be shamed before
my Lord and Master, if I did not declare his will in
regard to the uses of property. This question
passes over from one of private business, with which
I have no right to meddle, into the domain of public
safety, where I have a right to demand that places
which are fatal to the life and morals of the young
men and women of the town, shall not be encouraged
and allowed to flourish through the use of property
owned and controlled by men of influence in the
community, and especially by the members of Christ's
body which he prayed might be without spot or
wrinkle or any defilement. My brother," Phillip
went on, after a painful pause, " before God, in whose

presence we shall stand at last, am I not right in my view of this matter? Would not Christ say to you just what I am now saying?"

Mr. Bentley shrugged his shoulders and said something about not trying to mix up business and religion. Phillip sat looking at the man, reading him through and through, his heart almost bursting in him at the thought of what a man would do for the sake of money. At last he saw that he would gain nothing by prolonging the argument. He rose, and with the same sweet frankness which characterized his opening of the subject, he said, "Brother, I wish to tell you that it is my intention to speak of this matter next Sunday, in the first of my talks on Christ and Modern Society. I believe it is something he would talk about in public, and I will speak of it as I think he would."

"You must do your duty, of course, Mr. Strong," replied Mr. Bentley, somewhat coldly; and Phillip went out, feeling as if he had grappled with his first dragon in Milton, and found him to be a very ugly one and hard to kill. What hurt him as much as the lack of spiritual fineness of apprehension of evil in his church-member, was the knowledge that, as Mr. Bentley so carelessly put it, his salary was largely paid out of the rentals of those vile abodes. He grew sick at heart as he dwelt upon the disagreeable fact; and as he came back to the parsonage and went up to his cosey study, he groaned to think that it was supported by the money that men paid for the ruin of their souls.

"And this, because society is as it is!" he exclaimed, as he buried his face in his hands and leaned his elbows on his desk, while his cheeks flushed and his heart quivered at the thought of the filth and vileness the money had seen and heard which paid for the very desk at which he wrote his sermons.

But Phillip Strong was not one to give way at the first feeling of seeming defeat. Neither did he harshly condemn his members. He wondered at their lack of spiritual life ; but, to his credit be it said, he did not harshly condemn. Only, as Sunday approached, he grew more clear in his own mind as to his duty in the matter. Expediency whispered to him, "Better wait. You have just come here. The people like you now. To launch out into a crusade against this thing immediately, will only cause unpleasant feelings, and do no good. There are so many of your members involved that it will certainly alienate their support, and possibly lead to your losing your place as pastor, if it do not drive away the most influential members."

To all this plea of expediency Phillip replied, "Get thee behind me, Satan!" He said to himself, he might as well let the people know what he was, at the very first. It was not necessary that he should be their pastor, if they would none of him. It was necessary that he preach the truth boldly. The one question he asked himself was, "Would Jesus Christ, if he were pastor of Calvary Church in Milton to-day, speak of the matter next Sunday, and speak regardless of all consequences?" Phillip asked the question honestly; and, after long prayer and much communion with his Divine Master, he said, "Yes, I believe he would." It is possible that he might have gained his end by working with his members in private. Another man might have pursued that method, and still have been a courageous, true minister. But this is the story of Phillip Strong, not of another man, and this is what *he* did.

When Sunday morning came, he went into his pulpit with the one thought in mind, that he would simply and frankly, in his presentation of the subject, use the language and the spirit of his Master. He had seen several other property owners during the week, and his interviews were nearly all similar to the one with Mr. Bentley. He had not been able to see Mr. William Winter, the chairman of the trustees, as he had not returned home until very late Saturday night. Phillip saw him come into the church that morning, just as the choir rose to sing the anthem. He was a large, fine-looking man. Phillip admired his physical appearance, as he marched down the aisle to his pew, which was the third from the front, directly before the pulpit.

When the hymn had been sung, the offering taken, the prayer made, Phillip stepped out at one side of the pulpit and reminded the congregation that, according to his announcement of a week before, he would give the first of his series of monthly talks on Christ and Modern Society. His subject this morning, he said, was "The Right and Wrong Uses of Property."

He started out with the statement, which he claimed was verified everywhere in the word of God, that all property that men acquire is really only in the nature of trust funds, which the property holder is in duty bound to use as a steward. The gold is God's. The silver is God's. The cattle on a thousand hills. All land and water privileges and all the wealth of the earth and of the seas belong primarily to the Lord of all the earth. When any of this property comes within the control of a man, he is not at liberty to use it as if it were his own, and his alone, but as God would have him use it, to better the condition of life, and make men and communities happier and more useful.

From this statement Phillip went on to speak of the common idea which men had, that wealth and houses and lands were their own, to do with as they pleased; and he showed what misery and trouble had always flowed out of this great falsehood, and how nations and individuals were to-day in the greatest distress, because of the wrong uses to which God's property was put by men who had control of it. It was easy then to narrow the argument to the condition of affairs in Milton. As he stepped from the general to the particular, and began to speak of the rental of saloons and houses of gambling from property owners in Milton, and then characterized such a use of God's property as wrong and unchristian, it was curious to note the effect on the congregation. Men who had been listening complacently to Phillip's eloquent but quiet statements, as long as

he confined himself to historical facts, suddenly
became aware that the tall, noble-faced, resolute
and loving young preacher up there was talking right
at them ; and more than one mill-owner, merchant,
real-estate dealer, and even professional man, writhed
inwardly, and nervously shifted in his cushioned pew,
as Phillip spoke in the plainest terms of the terrible
example set the world by the use of property for
purposes which were destructive to all true society,
and a shame to civilization and Christianity.   Phillip
controlled his voice and his manner admirably, but
he drove the truth home and spared not.   His voice
at no time rose above a quiet conversational tone,
but it was clear, and his utterance was distinct.
The audience sat hushed in the spell of a genuine
sensation as Phillip went on; and the sensation
deepened when, at the close of a tremendous sentence, which swept through the church like a red-
hot flame, Mr. Winter suddenly arose in his pew,
passed out into the aisle, and walked deliberately
down and out of the door.   Phillip saw him and
knew the reason, but went straight on with his
message, and no one, not even his anxious wife, who
endured martyrdom for him that morning, could
detect any disturbance in Phillip from the mill-
owner's contemptuous withdrawal.

When Phillip closed with a prayer of tender
appeal that the Spirit of Truth would make all
hearts to behold the truth as one soul, the audience
remained seated longer than usual, still under the
influence of the subject, and the morning's sensa-

tional service. All through the day Phillip felt a
certain strain on him, which did not subside even
when the evening service was over. Very many of
the members, notably several of the mothers, thanked
him, with tears in their eyes, for his morning message.
Very few of the men talked with him. Mr. Winter
did not come out to the evening service, although he
was one of the very few men members who were
invariably present. Phillip noted his absence but
preached with his usual enthusiasm. He thought a
larger number of strangers was present than he had
seen the Sunday before. He was very tired when
the day was over.

The next morning, as he was getting ready to go
out for a visit to one of the mills, the bell rang.
He was near the door and opened it. There stood
Mr. Winter. " I should like to see you a few
moments, Mr. Strong, if you can spare the time,"
said the mill-owner, without offering to take the
hand Phillip extended.

" Certainly. Will you come up to my study?"
asked Phillip, quietly.

The two men went upstairs, and Phillip shut the
door, as he motioned Mr. Winter to a seat, and then
sat down opposite.

CHAPTER II.

"I HAVE come to see you about your sermon of yesterday morning," began Mr. Winter, abruptly. "I consider what you said was a direct insult to me personally."

"Suppose I should say it was not so intended," replied Phillip, with a good-natured smile.

"Then I should say you lied!" retorted Mr. Winter, sharply.

Phillip sat very still. And the two men eyed each other in silence for a moment. Then the minister reached out his hand, and laid it on the other's arm, saying as he did so, "My brother, you certainly did not come into my house to accuse me unjustly of wronging you? I am willing to talk the matter over in a friendly spirit, but will not listen to personal abuse."

There was something in the tone and manner of this declaration that subdued the mill-owner. He was an older man than Phillip by twenty years, but a man of quick and ungoverned temper. He had come to see the minister while in a heat of passion, and the way Phillip received him, the calmness and dignity of his attitude, thwarted his purpose. He wanted to find a man ready to quarrel. Instead, he found a man ready to talk reason. Mr. Winter replied, after a pause, during which he controlled himself by a great effort : —

" I consider that you purposely selected me as guilty of conduct unworthy a church-member and a Christian, and made me the target of your remarks yesterday. And I wish to say that such preaching will never do in Calvary Church while I am one of its members."

" Of course you refer to the matter of renting your property to saloon men and to halls for gambling and other evil uses," said Phillip, bluntly. " Are you the only member of Calvary Church who lets his property for such purposes ? "

" It is not a preacher's business to pry into the affairs of his church-members ! " replied Mr. Winter, growing more excited again. " That is what I object to."

" In the first place, Mr. Winter," said Phillip, steadily, " let us settle the right and wrong of the whole business. Is it right for a business man, a Christian man, a church-member, to rent his property for saloons and vicious resorts, where human life is ruined ? "

" That is not the question."

" What is ? " Phillip asked, with his eyes wide open.

Mr. Winter answered sullenly : " The question is whether our business affairs, those of other men with me, are to be dragged into the Sunday church-services, and made the occasion of personal attacks upon us. I for one will not sit and listen to any such preaching."

" But aside from the matter of private business, Mr. Winter, let us settle whether what you and others are doing is right. Will you let the other matter rest a moment, and tell me what is the duty of a Christian in the use of his property?"

" It is my property, and if I or my agent choose to rent it to another man in a legal, business-like way, that is my affair. I do not recognize that you have anything to do with it."

" Not if I am convinced that you are doing what is harmful to the community and to the church?"

" You have no business to meddle in our private affairs!" replied Mr. Winter, angrily. " And if you intend to pursue that method of preaching, I shall withdraw my support, and most of the influential, paying members will follow my example."

It was a cowardly threat on the part of the excited mill-owner, and it roused Phillip more than if he had been physically slapped in the face. If there was anything in all the world that stirred Phillip to his oceanic depths of feeling, it was an intimation that he was in the ministry for pay, and so must be afraid of losing the support of those members who were able to pay largely. He clenched his hands around the arms of his study-chair until his nails bent on the hard wood. His scorn and indignation burned in his face, although his voice was calm enough.

" Mr. Winter, this whole affair is a matter of the most profound principle with me. As long as I live I shall believe that a Christian man has no more right to rent his property to a saloon than he has to run a saloon himself. And as long as I live I shall also believe that it is a minister's duty to preach to his church plainly upon matters which bear upon the right and wrong of life, no matter what is involved in those matters. Are money and houses and lands of such a character that the use of them has no bearing on moral questions, and is therefore to be left out of the preaching material of the pulpit? It is my conviction that the men of property in this age have come to regard their business as separated and removed from God and all relation to Him. The business men of to-day do not regard their property as God's. They always speak of it as theirs. And they resent any ' interference,' as you call it, on the part of the pulpit. Nevertheless, I say it plainly, I regard the renting of these houses by you, and other business men in the church, to the whiskey men and the corrupters of youth as wholly wrong, and so wrong that the Christian minister who should keep silent when he knew the facts would be guilty of unspeakable cowardice and disloyalty to his Lord. As to your threat of withdrawal of support, sir, do you suppose I would be in the ministry if I were afraid of the rich men in my congregation? It shows that you are not yet acquainted with me. It would not hurt you to know me better ! ''

All the time Phillip was talking, his manner was that of dignified indignation. His anger was never · coarse or vulgar. But when he was roused as he was now he spoke with a total disregard for all consequences. For the time being he felt as perhaps one of the old Hebrew prophets used to feel when the flame of inspired wrath burned in his soul.

The man who sat opposite was compelled to keep silent until Phillip had said what he had to say. It was impossible for him to interrupt. Also it was out of the question that a man like Mr. Winter should understand a nature like that of Phillip Strong. The mill-owner sprang to his feet as soon as Phillip finished. He was white to the lips with passion, and so excited that his hands trembled and his voice shook as he replied to Phillip : —

"You shall answer for these insults, sir. I withdraw my church pledge, and you will see whether the business men in the church will sustain such preaching." And Mr. Winter flung himself out of the study and downstairs, forgetting to take his hat, which he had carried up with him. Phillip caught it up and went downstairs with it, reaching the mill-owner just as he was going out of the front door. He said simply, "You forgot your hat, sir." Mr. Winter took it without a word and went out, slamming the door hard behind him.

Phillip turned around, and there stood his wife. Her face was very anxious.

"Tell me all about it, Phillip," she said. Sunday evening they had talked over the fact of Mr. Winter's walking out of the church during the service, and had anticipated some trouble. Phillip related the facts of Mr. Winter's visit, telling his wife what the mill-owner had said.

"What did you say, Philip, to make him so angry? Did you give him a piece of your mind?"

"I gave him the whole of it," replied Phillip, somewhat grimly, — "at least all of it on that particular subject that he could stand."

"Oh, dear! It seems too bad to have this trouble come so soon! What will Mr. Winter do? He is very wealthy, and influential in the church. Do you think — are you sure you have done just right, for the best in this matter, Phillip? It is going to be very unpleasant for you."

"Well, Sarah, I would not do otherwise than I have done. What *have* I done? I have simply preached God's truth, as I plainly see it, to my church. And if I do not do that, what business have I in the ministry at all? I regret this personal encounter with Mr. Winter; but I don't see how I could have avoided it."

"Did you lose your temper?"

"No."

"There was some very loud talking. I could hear it away out in the kitchen."

"Well, you know, Sarah, the angrier I get the less inclined I feel to 'holler.' It was Mr. Winter you heard. He was very much excited when he came, and nothing that I could conscientiously say would have made any difference with him."

"Did you ask him to pray over the matter with you?"

"No. I do not think he was in a praying mood."

"Were you?"

Phillip hesitated a moment, and then replied seriously: "Yes, I truly believe I was, — that is, I should not have been ashamed at any part of the interview to put myself into loving communion with my Heavenly Father."

Mrs. Strong still looked disturbed and anxious. She was going over in her mind the probable result of Mr. Winter's antagonism to the minister. It looked to her like a very serious thing. Phillip was inclined to treat the affair with a calm philosophy, based on the knowledge that his conscience was clear of all fault in the matter.

"What do you suppose Mr. Winter will do?" Mrs. Strong asked.

"He threatened to withdraw his financial support, and said other paying members would do the same."

"Do you think they will?"

"I don't know. I should n't wonder if they did."

"What will you do then? It will be dreadful to have a disturbance of that kind in the church, Phillip; it will ruin your prospects here. You will not be able to work under all that friction."

And the minister's wife suddenly broke down and had a good cry; while Phillip comforted her, first by saying two or three funny things, and secondly by asserting, with a positive cheerfulness which was peculiar to him when he was hard pressed, that, even if the church withdrew all support, he could probably get a job somewhere on a railroad, or in a hotel, where there was always a demand for porters who could walk up several flights of stairs with a good-sized trunk.

" Sometimes I almost think I missed my calling," said Phillip, purposely talking about himself in order to make his wife come to the defence. " I ought to have been a locomotive fireman."

" The idea, Phillip Strong ! A man who has the gift of reaching people with preaching the way you do ! "

" The way I reach Mr. Winter, for example ! "

" Yes," said his wife, " the way you reach him. Why, the very fact that you made such a man angry is pretty good proof that you reached him. Such men are not touched by any ordinary preaching."

" So you really think I have a little gift at preaching ? " asked Philip, slyly.

" A little gift ! It is a great deal more than a little, Phillip."

" Are n't you a little prejudiced, Sarah ? "

" No, sir. I am the severest critic you ever have in the congregation. If you only knew how nervous you sometimes make me ! — when you get started on some exciting passage and make a gesture that would throw a stone image into a fit, and then begin to speak of something in a different way, like another person, and the first I know I am caught up and hurled into the subject, and forget all about you."

" Thank you," said Phillip.

" What for? " asked his wife, laughing. " For forgetting you? "

" I would rather be forgotten by you than remembered by any one else," replied Phillip, gallantly. " And you are such a delightful little flatterer that I feel courage for anything that may happen."

" It 's not flattery; it 's truth, Phillip. I do believe in you and your work; and I am only anxious that you should succeed here. I can't bear to think of trouble in the church. It would almost kill me to go through such times as we sometimes read about."

" We must leave results with God. I am sure we are not responsible for more than our utmost doing and living of necessary truth." Phillip spoke courageously.

" Then you don't feel disheartened by the event of this morning, Phillip? "

" No, I don't know that I do. I 'm very sensitive, and I feel hurt at Mr. Winter's threat of withdrawing financial support; but I don't feel disheartened for the work. Why should I? Am I not doing my best? "

" I believe you are. Only, dear Phillip, be wise. Do not try to reform everything in a week, or expect people to grow their wings before they have started even the pinfeathers. It is n't natural."

" Well, I won't," replied Phillip, with a laugh. " Better trim your wings, Sarah; they 're dragging on the floor."

He hunted up his hat (which was one of the

things Phillip could never find twice in the same place), kissed his wife, and went out to make the visit at the mill which he was getting ready to make when Mr. Winter called.

To his surprise, when he went down through the business part of the town, he discovered that his sermon of Sunday had roused almost every one. People were talking about it on the street, — an almost unheard-of way of treating sermons in Milton. When the evening paper came out it described in sensational paragraphs the Rev. Mr. Strong's attack on the wealthy sinners of his own church, and went on to say that the church " was very much wrought up over the sermon, and would probably make it uncomfortable for the reverend gentleman." Phillip wondered, as he read, at the unusual stir made because a preacher of Christ had denounced an undoubted evil.

" Is it, then," he asked himself, " such a remarkable piece of news that a minister of the gospel has preached from his own pulpit against what is without question an unchristian use of property? What is the meaning of the pulpit unless it exists to preach the Christianity of Christ applied to the uses of property, as well as to the uses of time and talent? Is it possible that the public is so little accustomed to hear anything on this subject that when they do hear it it is to them of the nature of sensational news? "

He pondered over these questions as he quietly but rapidly went along with his work that week. He was conscious as the days went on that trouble was brewing for him. He had met Mr. Winter several times on the street, and the mill-owner had not recognized him. This hurt him in a way hard to explain; but his sensitive spirit felt the cut like a lash on a sore place.

When Sunday came Phillip went into his pulpit and faced the largest audience he had yet seen in Calvary Church. As is often the case, people who had heard of his previous sermon on Sunday thought he would preach another like it. Instead of that he preached a sermon on the love of God for the world. In one way the large audience was disappointed. It had come to have its love of sensation fed, and Phillip had not given it anything of the kind. In another way the audience was profoundly moved by the power and sweetness of Phillip's unfolding of the great subject. Men who had not been inside of a church for years went away thoughtfully impressed with the old truth of God's love, and asked themselves what they had done to deserve it, — the very thing that Phillip wanted them to ask. The property-owners in the church who had felt offended by Phillip's sermon of the Sunday before went away from the service acknowledging that the new pastor was an eloquent preacher and a man of large gifts. In the evening Phillip preached again from the same theme, treating it in an entirely different way. His audience nearly filled the church, and was evidently deeply impressed.

In spite of all this, Phillip felt that a certain ele-

ment in the church had arrayed itself against him.
Mr. Winter did not appear at either service. There
were several other absences on the part of men who
had been constant attendants on the Sunday services. He felt, without hearing it, that a great deal
was being said in opposition to him; but, with the
burden of it beginning to oppress him a little, he
saw nothing better to do than to go on with his
work as if nothing unusual had taken place.

Pursuing the plan he had originally mapped out
when he came to Milton, he spent much of his time
in the afternoons studying the social and civic life
of the town. As the first Sunday of the next month
drew near, when he was to speak again on the attitude of Christ in respect to some practices of modern society, he determined to select the saloon as
one of the prominent features of modern life that
would naturally be noticed by Christ, and doubtless
be denounced by him as a great evil.

In his study of the saloon question he did a thing
which he had never done before, and then only after
very much deliberation and prayer. He went into
the saloons themselves on different occasions. He
wanted to know from actual knowledge what sort of
places the saloons were. What he saw after a dozen
visits to as many different groggeries added fuel to
the flame of indignation that already burned hot in
him. The sight of the vast army of men turning
into beasts in these dens created in him a loathing
and a hatred of the whole iniquitous institution that
language failed to express. He wondered with un-

speakable astonishment in his soul that a civilized community in the nineteenth century would tolerate for one moment the public sale of an article that led, on the confession of society itself, to countless crimes against the law of the land and of God. His indignant astonishment deepened yet more, if that were possible, when he found that the license of five hundred dollars a year for each saloon was used by the town to support its public-school system. That, to Phillip's mind, was an awful sarcasm on Christian civilization. It seemed to him like selling a man poison according to law, and then taking the money from the sale to help the widow to purchase mourning. It was fully as ghastly as that would be.

He went to see some of the other ministers, hoping to unite them in a combined attack on the saloon power. It seemed to him that, if the Church as a whole entered the crusade against the saloon, it could be driven out even from Milton, where it had been so long established. To his surprise he found the other churches unwilling to unite in a public battle against the whiskey men. Several of the ministers openly defended license as the only practicable method of dealing with the saloon. All of them confessed it was evil, and only evil, but under the circumstances thought it would do little good to agitate the subject. Phillip came away from several interviews with the ministers, sad and sick at heart. He was too frank and open-hearted himself to see, what was a fact, that some of the other preachers were jealous of his popularity, and had taken offence because Phillip had drawn away people from their own services, especially to his Sunday night meetings.

He approached several of the prominent men in the town, hoping to enlist some of them in the fight against the rum power. Here he met with unexpected opposition, coming in a form he had not anticipated. One prominent citizen said : —

" Mr. Strong, you will ruin your chances here if you attack the saloons in this savage manner; and I 'll tell you why : The whiskey men hold a tremendous influence in Milton in the matter of political power. The city election comes off the middle of next month. The men up for office are dependent for election on the votes of the saloon men and their following. You will cut your head off sure if you come out against them in public. Why, there 's Mr. ——, and ——, and So-and-So " (he named half a dozen men) " in your church who are up for office in the coming election. They can't be elected without the votes of the rummies, and they know it. Better steer clear of it, Mr. Strong. The saloon has been a regular thing in Milton for over fifty years ; it is as much a part of the town as the churches or schools ; and I tell you it is a power ! "

" What ! " cried Phillip, in unbounded astonishment, " do you tell me, you, a leading citizen of the town of 80,000 immortal souls, that the saloon power here has its grip to this extent on the civic and social life of the place, and you are willing to sit down and let this devil of crime and ruin throttle you, and not raise a finger to change or expel the

monster? It is impossible! It is not consistent
with the character of Christian America that such a
state of affairs in our political life should be
endured!"

"Nevertheless," replied the business man, "these
are the facts. And you will simply dash your own
life out against a wall of solid rock if you try to fight
this evil. You have my warning."

"May I not also have your help!" cried Phillip,
hungry in his soul for companionship in the struggle
which he saw was coming.

"It would ruin my business to come out against
the saloon," replied the man, frankly.

"And what is that?" cried Phillip, earnestly. "It
has already ruined far more that ought to be dear
to you. Man, man, what are money and business
compared with your own flesh and blood? Do you
know where your own son was two nights ago? In
one of the vilest of the vile holes in this city, which
you, a father, license to another man to destroy the life
of your own child! I saw him there myself; and
my heart ached for him and you. Ah, brother, forgive me for wounding you! It is the necessary
truth. Will you join with me to wipe out this curse
to society?"

The merchant trembled and his lips quivered at
mention of his son, but he replied: —

"I cannot do what you want, Mr. Strong. But
you can count on my sympathy if you make the
fight." And Phillip finally went away, his soul
tossed on a wave of mountain proportions, which

was growing more and more crested with foam and wrath as the first Sunday of the month drew near, and he realized that the battle was one that he must wage single-handed in a town of eighty thousand people.

He was not so destitute of support as he thought. There were many mothers' hearts in Milton that had ached and prayed in agony long years that the Almighty would come with his power and sweep the curse away. But Phillip had not been long enough in Milton to know the sentiment of the entire people. He had so far touched only the Church, through its representative pulpits, and a few of the leading business men, and the result had been almost to convince him that very little help could be expected from the public generally. He was appalled to find out what a tremendous hold the whiskey men had on the business and politics of the place. It was a revelation to him of their power. The whole thing seemed to him like a travesty of free government, and a terrible commentary on the boasted Christianity of the century.

So when he walked into the pulpit the first Sunday of the month he felt his message burning in his heart and on his lips as never before. It seemed beyond all question that if Christ were pastor of Calvary Church he would speak out in plain denunciation of the whiskey power. And so, after the opening part of the service, Phillip rose to speak, facing an immense audience that overflowed the galleries and invaded the pulpit platform. Such a crowd had never been seen in Calvary Church before.

Phillip had not announced his subject, but there was an expectation on the part of many that he was going to denounce the "rummies." In the two months that Phillip had been preaching in Milton he had attracted great attention. His audience this morning represented a great many different kinds of people. Some came out of curiosity. Others came because the crowd was going that way. So it happened that Phillip faced a truly representative audience of Milton people. As his eye swept over the house he saw four of the six members of his church who were up for office at the coming election.

For an hour Phillip spoke as he had never spoken in all his life before. His subject, the cause it represented, the immense audience, the entire occasion caught him up in a genuine burst of eloquent fury, and his sermon swept through the house like a prairie fire driven by a high gale. At the close, he spoke of the power of the Church compared with that of the saloon, and showed how easily it could win the victory against any kind of evil if it were only united and determined.

" Men and women of Milton, fathers, mothers, and citizens," he said, " this evil is one which cannot be driven out unless the Christian people of this place unite to condemn it, regardless of results. It is too firmly established. It has its clutch on business, the municipal life, and even the Church itself. It is a fact that the Church in Milton has

4

been afraid to take the right stand in this matter. Members of the churches have become involved in the terrible entanglement of the long-established rum-power, until to-day you witness a condition of affairs which ought to stir the righteous indignation of every citizen and father. What is it you are enduring? An institution which blasts with its poisonous breath every soul that enters it, which ruins young manhood, which kills more citizens in times of peace than the most bloody war ever slew in times of revolution; an institution that has not one good thing to commend it; an institution that is established for the open and declared purpose of getting money from the people by the sale of stuff that creates criminals; an institution that robs the honest working-man of his savings, and looks with indifference on the tears of the wife or the sobs of the mother; an institution that never gives one cent of its enormous wealth to build churches, colleges, or homes for the needy; an institution that has the brand of the murderer, the harlot, and the gambler burned into it with a brand of the Devil's own forging in the furnace of his hottest hell, — this institution so rules and governs this town of Milton to-day that honest citizens tremble before it, business men dare not oppose it for fear of losing money, church-members fawn upon it in order to gain place in politics, and ministers of the gospel confront its hideous insolence, and say nothing! It is high time we faced this monster of iniquity and drove it out of the stronghold it has occupied so long.

"I wish you could have gone with me this past week and witnessed some of the sights I have seen. No! I retract that statement. I would not wish that any father or mother had had the heartache that I have felt as I contemplated the ruins of young lives crumbling into the decay of premature debility, mocking the manhood that God gave them by yielding themselves slaves to their passions and degrading themselves below the beasts that perish. What have I seen? O ye fathers! O ye mothers! Do you know what is going on in this place of sixty saloons licensed by your own act and made legal by your own will? Yes, madam, and you, sir, who have covenanted together in the fellowship and discipleship of the purest institution of God on earth, who have sat here in front of this pulpit and partaken of the emblems which remind you of your Redeemer, where are your sons, your brothers, your lovers, your friends? They are not here this morning. The Church has not any hold on them. They are growing up to disregard the duties of good citizenship. They are walking down the broad avenue of destruction, and what is this town doing to prevent it? I have seen young men from what we call the best homes in this town reel in and out of gilded temples of evil, oaths on their lips and passion in their looks, and the cry of my soul has gone up to Almighty God that the Church and the Home might combine their mighty force to drive the whiskey demon out of our municipal life so that we might never feel the curse again evermore.

"I speak to you to-day in the name of my Lord and Master. It is impossible for me to believe that if the Christ of God were standing here this morning he would advise the licensing of this corruption as the most feasible or expedient method of dealing with it. I cannot imagine him using the argument that the saloon must be licensed for the revenue that may be gained from it to support the school system. I cannot imagine Christ taking any other position before the whiskey power than that of uncompromising condemnation. He would say it is evil and only evil, and therefore to be opposed by every legal and moral restriction that society could rear against it. In his name, speaking as I believe he would speak if he were here this moment, I solemnly declare the necessity on the part of every disciple of Christ in every church in Milton of placing himself decidedly and persistently and at once in open battle against the saloon until it is destroyed, until its power in business, politics, and society is a thing of the past, until we have rid ourselves of the foul viper which has so many years trailed its slimy folds through our homes and our schools.

"Citizens, Christians, church-members, I call on you to-day to take arms against the common foe of all that we hold dear in church, home, and state. I know there are honest business men who have long writhed in secret at the ignominy of the halter about their necks by which they have been led. There are citizens who have the best interests of the community at heart who have hung their heads in shame of American politics, seeing this brutal whiskey element dictating the government of the town, and parcelling out its patronage and managing its funds and enormous stealings of the people's money. I know there are church-members who have felt in their hearts the deep shame of bowing the knee to this rum god in order to make advancement in political life. And I call on all these to-day to rise with me and begin a fight against the entire saloon business and whiskey rule in Milton until by the help of the Lord of hosts we have gotten us the victory. Men, women, brothers, sisters in the great family of God on earth, will you sit tamely down and worship the great beast of this century! Will you not rather gird your swords upon your thighs and go out to battle against this blasphemous Philistine who has defied the armies of the living God? I have spoken my message. Let us ask divine wisdom and power to help us."

Phillip's prayer was almost painful in its intensity of feeling and expression. The audience sat in deathly silence, and when he pronounced the amen of the benediction it was several moments before any one stirred to leave the church.

Phillip went home completely exhausted by his effort. He had put into his sermon all of himself and had called up all his reserve power, — a thing he was not often guilty of doing, and for which he condemned himself on this occasion. But it was past, and he could not recall it. He was not concerned as to the results of his sermon. He had

long believed that if he spoke the message God gave
him he was not to grow anxious over the outcome
of it.

But the people of Milton were deeply stirred by
the address. They were not accustomed to hear
that kind of preaching. And what was more, the
whiskey element was roused. It was not accustomed
to have its authority attacked in that bold, almost
savage manner. For years its sway had been un-
disputed. It had insolently established itself in
power until even those citizens who knew its thoroughly evil character were deceived into the belief
that nothing better than licensing it was possible.
The idea that the saloon could be banished, removed, driven out altogether, had never before been
advocated in Milton. The conviction that it could
be and ought to be suppressed had never gained
ground with any number of people. They had endured it as a necessary evil. Phillip's sermon
therefore fell something like a bomb into the whiskey
camp. Before night the report of the sermon had
spread all over the town. The saloon men were
enraged. Ordinarily they would have paid no attention to anything a church or a preacher might
say or do. But Phillip spoke from the pulpit of the
largest church in Milton. The whiskey men knew
that if the large churches should all unite to fight
them they would make matters very uncomfortable
for them and in the end probably drive them out.
Phillip went home that Sunday night after the evening service with several bitter enemies. The whiskey

men constituted one element. Some of his own
church-members made up another. He had struck
again at the same sore spot which he had wounded
the month before. In his attack on the saloon as
an institution he had again necessarily condemned
all those members of his church who rented property to the whiskey element or had dealings with
them in business. Again, as a month ago, these
property holders went from the hearing of Phillip's
sermon angry that they as well as the saloon power
were under indictment.

As Phillip entered on the week's work after that
eventful sermon of the first of the month he began
to feel the pressure of public feeling against him.
He began to realize the bitterness of championing a
just cause alone. He felt the burden of the community's sin in the matter, and more than once he
felt obliged to come in from his parish work and go
up into his study there to commune with his Father.
He was growing old very fast during those first few
weeks in his new parish.

Tuesday evening of that week Phillip had been
writing a little while in his study, where he had gone
immediately after supper. It was nearly eight o'clock
when he happened to remember that he had promised a sick child in the home of one of his parish-
ioners that he would come and see him that very
day.

He came downstairs, put on his hat and over-
coat, and told his wife where he was going.

" It 's not far. I shall be back in about half an
hour, Sarah."

He went out, and his wife held the door open until he was down the steps. She was just on the point of shutting the door as Phillip started down the walk of the street, when a sharp report rang out close by. She screamed and flung the door open again, as by the light of the street lamp she saw Phillip stagger and then leap into the street toward an elm-tree which grew almost opposite the parsonage. When he was about in the middle of the street the minister's wife was horrified to see a man step out boldly from behind the tree, raise a gun, and deliberately fire at Phillip again. This time Phillip fell and did not rise. His tall form lay where the rays of the street lamp shone on it and he had fallen so that as his arms stretched out there he made the figure of a huge and prostrate cross.

CHAPTER III.

AS people waked up in Milton the Wednesday morning after the shooting of Phillip Strong they grew conscious of the fact, as the news came to their knowledge, that they had been nursing for fifty years one of the most brutal and cowardly institutions on earth, and licensing it to do the very thing which at last it had done. For the time being Milton suffered a genuine shock. Long pent-up feeling against the whiskey power burst out, and public sentiment for once condemned the source of the cowardly attempt to murder.

Various rumors were flying about. It was said that Mr. Strong had been stabbed in the back while out making parish calls in company with his wife, and that she had been wounded by a pistol-shot herself. It was also said that Phillip had been shot through the heart and instantly killed. But all these confused reports were finally set at rest when those calling at the parsonage brought away the exact truth.

The first shot fired by the man from behind the tree struck Phillip in the knee but the ball glanced off. Phillip felt the blow and staggered, but his next impulse was to rush in the direction of the sound and disarm his assailant. That was the reason he had leaped into the street. But the second shot was better aimed and the bullet crashed into his upper arm and shoulder, shattering the bone and producing an exceedingly painful though not fatal wound.

The shock caused Phillip to fall as if dead, and he fainted away, but not before the face of the man who had shot him was clearly stamped on his mind. He knew that he was one of the saloon proprietors whose establishment Phillip had visited the week before. He was a man with a hare-lip, and there was no mistaking his countenance.

When the people of Milton learned that Phillip was not fatally wounded their excitement cooled a little. A wave of indignation, however, swept over the town when it was learned that the would-be murderer was recognized by the minister, and it was rumored that he had openly threatened that he would "fix the cursed preacher so that he would not be able to preach again."

Phillip, however, felt more full of fight against the great rum-devil than ever. As he lay on the bed the morning after the shooting he had nothing to regret or fear. The surgeon had been called at once, as soon as his wife and the alarmed neighbors had been able to carry him into the parsonage. The ball had been removed and the wounds dressed. By noon Phillip had recovered somewhat from the effects of the operation and was resting, although very weak from the shock and suffering considerable pain.

"What is that stain on the floor, Sarah?" he asked as his wife came in with some article for his comfort. Phillip lay where he could see into the other room.

"It is your blood, Phillip," replied his wife, with a shudder. "It flowed like a stream from your shoulder as we carried you in last night. O Phillip, it is dreadful! It seems to me like an awful nightmare. Let us move away from this terrible place. You will be killed if we stay here!"

"There isn't much danger if the rest of 'em are as poor shots as this fellow," replied Phillip. "Now, little woman," he went on cheerfully, "don't worry. I don't believe they'll try it again."

Mrs. Strong controlled herself. She did not want to break down while Phillip was in his present condition.

"You must not talk," she said as she smoothed his hair back from the pale forehead.

"That's pretty hard on a preacher, don't you think, Sarah? My occupation is gone if I can't talk."

"Then I'll talk for two. They say that most women can do it."

"Will you preach for me next Sunday?"

"What, and make myself a target for saloon-keepers? No, thank you. I have half a mind to forbid your ever preaching again. It will be the death of you."

"It is the life of me, Sarah. I would not ask anything better than to die with the armor on, fighting evil. Well, all right. I won't talk any more. I suppose there's no objection to my thinking a little?"

"Thinking is the worst thing you can do. You just want to lie there and do nothing but get well."

"All right. I'll quit everything except eating and sleeping. Put up a little placard on the head of the bed saying, 'Biggest curiosity in Milton! A live minister who has stopped thinking and talking! Admission ten cents. Proceeds to be devoted to teach saloon-keepers how to shoot straight." Phillip was still somewhat under the influence of the doctor's anæsthetic, and as he faintly murmured this absurd sentence he fell into a slumber which lasted several hours, from which he awoke very feeble, and realizing that he would be confined to the house several weeks, but feeling in good spirits and thankful out of the depths of his vigorous nature that he was still spared to do God's will on earth.

The next day he felt strong enough to receive a few visitors. Among them was the chief of police, who came to inquire concerning the identity of the man who had done the shooting. Phillip showed some reluctance to witness against his enemy. It was only when he remembered that he owed a duty to society as well as to himself that he described the man and related minutely the entire affair exactly as it occurred.

"Is the man in town?" asked Phillip. "Has he not fled?"

"I think I know where he is," replied the officer. "He is hiding, but I can find him. In fact we have been hunting for him since the shooting. He is wanted on several other charges."

Phillip was pondering something in silence. At last he said : —

"When you have arrested him I wish you would bring him here if it can be done without violating any ordinance or statute."

The officer stared at the request, and the minister's wife exclaimed, "Phillip, you will not have that man come into the house ! Besides, you are not well enough to endure a meeting with the wretch ! "

"Sarah, I have a good reason for it. Really, I am well enough. You will bring him, won't you? I do not wish to make any mistake in the matter. Before the man is really confined under a criminal charge of attempt to murder I should like to confront him here. There can be no objection to that, can there?"

The officer finally promised that, if he could do so without attracting too much attention, he would comply with Phillip's request. It was a thing he had never done before ; he was not quite easy in his mind about it. Nevertheless, Phillip exercised a winning influence over all sorts and conditions of men, and he felt quite sure that, if the officer could arrest his man quietly, he would bring him to the parsonage.

This was Thursday night. The next evening, just after dark, the bell rang, and one of the church-.

members who had been staying with Mrs. Strong
during the day went to the door. There stood two
men. One of them was the chief of police. He
inquired how the minister was, and said that he had
a man with him whom the minister was anxious to
see.

Phillip heard them talking, and guessed who they
were. He sent his wife out to have the men come
in. The officer with his man came into the bed-
room where Phillip lay, still weak and suffering, but
at his request propped up a little with pillows.

" Well, Mr. Strong, I have got the man, and here
he is," said the officer, wondering what Phillip could
want of him. " I ran him down in the 'crow's
nest' below the mills, and we popped him into a
hack and drove right up here with him. And a
pretty sweet specimen he is, I can tell you ! Take
off your hat and let the gentleman have another
look at the brave chap who fired at him in
ambush ! "

The officer spoke almost brutally, forgetting for a
moment that the prisoner's hands were manacled ;
remembering it the next instant, he pulled off the
man's hat, while Phillip looked calmly at the features. Yes, it was the same hideous, brutal face,
with the hare-lip, which had shown up in the rays of
the street-lamp that night ; there was no mistaking
it for any other.

" Why did you want to kill me ? " asked Phillip,
after a significant pause. " I never did you any
harm."

" I would like to kill all the cursed preachers,"
replied the man, hoarsely.

" You confess, then, that you are the man who
fired at me, do you?"

" I don't confess anything. What do you want to
talk to me for? Take me to the lock-up if you 're
going to!" the man exclaimed fiercely, turning to
the officer.

" Phillip!" cried his wife, turning to him with a
gesture of appeal, "send them away. It will do no
good to talk to this man."

Phillip raised his left hand in a gesture toward
the man that made every one in the room feel a
little awed. The officer in speaking of it afterward
said : " I tell you, boys, I never felt quite the same,
except once, when the old Catholic priest stepped
up on the platform with old man Gower time he
was hanged at Millville. Somehow then I felt as
if, when the priest raised his hand and began to say
his prayer, maybe we might all be glad to have some
one pray for us if we got into a tight place."

Phillip spoke directly to the man, whose look fell
beneath that of the minister.

" You know well enough that you are the man who
shot me Tuesday night. I know you are the man, for
I saw your face very plainly by the light of the street
lamp. Now, all that I wanted to see you here for
before you were taken to jail was to let you know
that I do not bear any hatred against you. The
act you have committed is against the law of God
and man. The injury you have inflicted against me

is very slight compared with that against your own soul. O my brother man, why should you try to harm me because I denounced your business? Do you not know in your heart of hearts that the saloon is so evil in its effects that a man who loves his home and his country must speak out against it? And yet I love you; that is possible because you are human. O my Father," Phillip continued, changing his appeal to the man, by an almost natural manner, into a petition to the Infinite, " make this soul, dear to thee, to behold thy love for him, and make him see that it is not against me, a man merely, that he has sinned, but against thyself, — against thy purity and holiness and affection. O my God, thou who didst come in the likeness of sinful man to seek and save that which was lost, stretch out the arms of thy salvation now to this child and save him from himself, from his own disbelief, or hatred of me, or of what I have said. Thou art all-merciful and all-loving. We leave all souls of men in the protecting, enfolding embrace of thy boundless compassion, of infinite grace."

There was a moment of entire quiet in the room, and then Phillip said faintly : " Sarah, I cannot say more. Only tell the man I bear him no hatred, and commend him to the love of God."

Mrs. Strong was alarmed at Phillip's appearance. The scene had been too much for his strength. She hastily commanded the officer to take his prisoner away, and with the help of her friend cared for the minister, who after the first faintness rallied, and then

gradually sank into sleep that proved more refresh-
ing than any he had yet enjoyed since the night of
the shooting.

The next day found Phillip improving more rapidly than Mrs. Strong had thought possible. She
forbade him the sight of all callers, however, and
insisted that he must keep quiet. His wounds were
healing satisfactorily, and when the surgeon called,
he expressed himself much pleased with his patient's
appearance.

" Say, doctor, do you really think it would set me
back any to think a little ? "

" No. I never heard of thinking hurting most
people ; I have generally considered it a healthy
habit."

" The reason I asked," continued Phillip, gravely,
" was that my wife absolutely forbade it, and I was
wondering how long I could keep it up and fool
anybody."

" That 's a specimen of his stubbornness, doctor,"
said the minister's wife, smilingly. " Why, only a
few minutes before you came in he was insisting
that he could preach to-morrow. Think of that ! —
a man with a shattered shoulder, who would have to
stand on one leg and do all his gesturing with his
left hand ! a man who can't preach without the use
of seven or eight arms, and as many pockets, and
has to walk up and down the platform like a lion
when he gets started in on his delivery ! And yet he
wants to preach to-morrow ! He 's so stubborn that
I don't know that I can keep him at home. You

5

had better leave some powders to put him to sleep, and we will keep him in a state of unconsciousness until Monday morning."

"Now, doctor, just listen to me a while. Mrs. Strong is talking for two women, as she agreed to do, and that puts me in a hard position. But I want to know how soon I can get to work again."

"You will have to lie there a month," said the doctor, bluntly.

"Impossible! I never lay that time in my life!" said Phillip, soberly.

"It would serve him right to perform a surgical operation on him for that, wouldn't it, Mrs. Strong?" the surgeon appealed to her.

"I think he deserves the worst you can do, doctor."

"But say, dear people, I can't stay here a month. I must be about my Master's business. What will the church do for supplies?"

"Don't worry, Phillip. The church will take care of that."

But Phillip was already eager to get to work. Only the assurance of the surgeon that he might possibly get out in a little over three weeks satisfied him. Sunday came and passed. Some one from a neighboring town who happened to be visiting in Milton occupied the pulpit, and Phillip had a quiet, restful day. He started in with the week determined to beat the doctor's time for recovery; and having a remarkably strong constitution and a tremendous will, he bade fair to be limping about the house in two weeks. His shoulder wound healed very fast. His knee bothered him and it seemed likely that he would go lame for a long time. But he was not concerned about that if only he could go about in any sort of fashion once more.

Wednesday of that week he was surprised in an unexpected manner by an event which did more than anything else to hasten his recovery. He was still confined to bed downstairs when in the afternoon the bell rang, and Mrs. Strong went to the door supposing it was one of the church people come to inquire about the minister. She found instead Alfred Burke, Phillip's old college chum and Seminary classmate. And in answer to his eager inquiry concerning Phillip's condition Mrs. Strong welcomed him heartily, as she brought him into Phillip's room, knowing her patient quite well enough to feel sure the sight of his old chum would do him more good than harm. The first thing that Alfred said was : —

" Old man, I hardly expected to see you again this side of heaven. How does it happen that you are alive here after all the times the papers had you killed ? "

" Bad marksmanship, principally. I used to think I was a big man. But after the shooting I came to the conclusion that I must be rather small."

" Your heart is so big it's a wonder to me that you were n't shot through it, no matter where you were hit. But I tell you it seems good to see you in the flesh once more."

"Why did n't you come and preach for me last Sunday?" said Phillip, quizzically.

"Why, have n't you heard? I did not get news of this affair until last Saturday in my far Western parish, and I was just in the throes of packing up to come on to Elmdale."

"Elmdale?"

"Yes, I 've had a call there. So we shall be near neighbors. Mrs. Burke is up there now getting the house straightened out, and I came right off down here."

"So you are pastor of the Chapel Hill Church? It 's a splendid opening for a young preacher. Congratulations, Alfred."

"Thank you, Phillip. By the way, I saw by the paper that you had declined a call to Elmdale, so I suppose they pitched on me for a second choice. You never wrote me of their call to you," he said, a little reproachfully.

"It did n't occur to me," replied Phillip, truthfully. "But how are you going to like it? Is n't it rather a dull old place?"

"Yes, I suspect it is, compared with Milton. I suppose you could n't live without the excitement of dodging assassins and murderers every time you go out to prayer meeting or parish calls. How do you like your work so far?"

"There is plenty of it," answered Phillip, gravely. "A minister must be made of cast-iron and fire-brick in order to stand the wear and tear of these times in which we live. I 'd like a week to trade ideas with you and talk over the work, Alfred."

"You 'd get the worst of the bargain."

"I don't know about that. I 'm not doing anything lately. But say, we 're going to be only fifty
miles apart; what 's to hinder an exchange once
in a while?"

"I 'm agreeable to that," replied Phillip's chum;
"on condition, however, that you furnish me with
a gun and pay all surgeons' bills when I occupy
your pulpit."

"Done," said Phillip, with a grin; and just then
Mrs. Strong forbade any more talk. Alfred stayed
until the evening train and when he left he stooped
down and kissed Phillip's cheek. "It 's a custom
we learned when we were in the German univer-
sities together that summer after college, you know,"
he explained with the slightest possible blush, when
Mrs. Strong came in and caught him in the act.
It seemed to her, however, like an affecting thing
that two big, grown-up men like her husband and
his old chum showed such tender affection for each
other. The love of men for men in the strong
friendship of school and college life is one of the
marks of human divinity.

In spite of his determination to get out and
occupy his pulpit the first Sunday of the next
month, Phillip was reluctantly obliged to let five
Sundays go by before he was able to preach. During those six weeks his attention was called to a
subject which he felt ought to be made the theme
of one of his talks on Christ and Modern Society.
The leisure which he had for reading opened his

eyes to the fact that the Sabbath in Milton was terribly desecrated. Shops of all kinds stood wide open. Excursion trains ran into the large city forty miles away, two theatres were always running with some variety show, and the saloons, in violation of an ordinance forbidding it, unblushingly flung their doors open and did more business on that day than any other. As Phillip read the papers he noticed that every Monday morning the police court was more crowded with "drunks" and "disorderlies" than on any other day in the week, and the plain cause of it was the abuse of the day before. In the summer time base-ball games were played in Milton on Sunday. In the fall and winter very many people spent their evenings in card-playing or aimlessly strolling up and down the main street. These facts came to Phillip's knowledge gradually, and he was not long in making up his mind that Christ would not keep silent before the facts. So he carefully prepared a plain statement of his belief in Christ's standing on the modern use of Sunday, and as on the other occasions when he had spoken the first Sunday in the month, he cast out of his reckoning all thought of the consequences. His one purpose was to do just as in his thought Christ would do with that subject.

The people in Milton thought that the first Sunday Phillip appeared in his pulpit he would naturally denounce the saloon again. But when he finally recovered sufficiently to preach again he determined that for a while he would say nothing in the way of sermons against the whiskey evil. He had a great horror of seeming to ride a hobby, of being a man of one idea and making people tired of him because he harped on one string. He had uttered his denunciation and he would wait a little before he spoke again. The whiskey power was not the only bad thing in Milton that needed to be attacked. There were other things which must be said. And so Phillip limped into his pulpit the third Sunday of the month and preached on a general theme, to the disappointment of a great crowd, almost as large as the last one he had faced. And yet his very appearance was a sermon in itself against the institution he had held up to public condemnation on that occasion. His knee wound proved very stubborn, and he limped badly. That in itself spoke eloquently of the dastardly attempt on his life. His face was pale and he had grown thin. His shoulder was stiff and the enforced quietness of his delivery contrasted strangely with his customary fiery appearance on the platform. Altogether that first Sunday of his reappearance in his pulpit was a stronger sermon against the saloon than anything he could have spoken or written.

When the first Sunday in the next month came on, Phillip was more like his old self. He had gathered strength enough to go around two Sunday afternoons and note for himself the desecration of the day as it went on recklessly. As he saw it all, it seemed to him that the church in Milton was practically doing nothing to stop the evil. All the ministers complained of the difficulty of getting an evening congregation. Yet hundreds of young people walked past all the churches every Sunday night, bent on pleasure, going to the theatres or concerts or parties, which seemed to have no trouble in attracting the crowd. Especially was this true of the foreign population, the working element connected with the mills. It was a common occurrence for dog fights, cock fights, and shooting matches of various kinds to be going on in the tenement district on Sunday, and the police seemed powerless or careless in the matter.

All this burned into Phillip like molten metal, and when he faced his people on the Sunday already becoming a noted Sunday for them, he quivered with the earnestness and thrill that always come to a sensitive man when he feels sure he has a sermon which must be preached and a message which the people must hear for their lives.

He took for a text Christ's words, " The Sabbath was made for man; " and at once defined its meaning as a special day.

"The true meaning of our modern Sunday may be summed up in two words, Rest and Worship. Under the head of Rest may be gathered whatever is needed for the people, and healthful recuperation of one's physical and mental powers, always regarding, not simply our own ease and comfort, but also the same right to rest on the part of the remainder of the community. Under the head of Worship may be gathered all those acts which either through dis-

tinct religious service or work tend to bring men
into closer and dearer relation to spiritual life, to
teach men larger, sweeter truths of existence, and
leave them better fitted to take up the duties of
every-day business.

" Now it is plain to me that if Christ were here
to-day, and pastor of Calvary Church, he would feel
compelled to say some very plain words about the
desecration of the Sabbath in Milton. Take for
example the opening of the fruit stands and cigar
stores and meat markets every Sunday morning.
What is the one reason why these places are open
this very minute while I am speaking? There is
only one reason, — in order that the owners of these
places may sell their goods and make money. They
are not satisfied with what they can make in six days.
Their greed seizes on the one day which ought to
be used for the rest and worship men need, and
turns that also into a day of merchandise. Do we
need any other fact to convince us of the terrible
selfishness of the human heart?

" Or take the case of the saloons. What right
have they to open their doors in direct contradiction
to the town ordinance forbidding it? And yet this
ordinance is held by them in such contempt that
this very morning as I came to this church I passed
more than half a dozen of these sections of hell,
wide open to any poor sinning soul that might be
enticed in there. Citizens of Milton, where does
the responsibility for this violation of law rest? Does
it rest with the churches and the preachers to see

that the few Sunday laws we have are enforced by them, while the business men and the police lazily dodge the issue and care not how the matter goes, saying it is none of their business?

"But suppose you say the saloons are beyond your power. That does not release you from doing what is in your power, easily, to prevent this day from being trampled under foot and made like every other day in its scramble after money and pleasure. Who own these fruit stores and cigar stands and meat markets, and who patronize them? Is it not true that church-members encourage all these places by purchasing of them on the Lord's Day? I have been told by one of these fruit dealers with whom I have talked lately that among his best customers on Sunday are some of the most respected members of this church. It has also been told me that in the summer time the heaviest patronage of the Sunday ice-cream business is from the church-members of Milton. Of what value is it that we place on our ordinance laws forbidding the sale of these things on Sunday, and then violate the statute by buying the very things covered by the law? How far are we responsible by our example for encouraging the breaking of the day on the part of those who would find it unprofitable to keep their business going if we did not purchase of them on this day?

"It is possible there are very many persons here in this house this morning who are ready to exclaim, 'This is intolerable bigotry and puritanical narrowness. This is not the attitude Christ would take on this question. He was too large-minded. He was too far advanced in thought to make the day mean anything of that sort.'

" But let us consider what is meant by the Sunday of our modern life as Christ would view it. There is no disputing the fact that the age is material, mercantile, money-making. For six feverish, eager, rushing days it is absorbed in the pursuit of money or fame or pleasure. Then God strikes the note of his silence in among the clashing sounds of earth's Babel and calls mankind to make a day unlike the other days. It is his merciful thoughtfulness for the race which has created this special day for men. Is it too much to ask that on this one day men think of something else besides politics, stocks, business, amusement? Is God grudging the man the pleasure of life when He gives the man six days for labor and then asks for only one day specially set apart for him? The objection to very many things commonly mentioned by the pulpit as harmful to Sunday is not necessarily based upon the harmfulness of the things themselves, but upon the fact that these things are repetitions of the working day, and so are distracting to the observance of the Sunday as a day of Rest and Worship, undisturbed by the things that have already for six days crowded the thought of men. Let me illustrate.

" Take for example the case of the Sunday paper, as it pours into Milton every Sunday morning on the special newspaper train. Now, there may not be anything in the contents of these Sunday papers that is any worse than can be found in any week-day edition. Granted, for the sake of the illustration, that the matter found in the Sunday paper is just like that in the Saturday issue, — politics, fashion, locals, personals, dramatic and sporting news, literary articles by well-known writers, a serial story, police record, crime, accident, fatality, etc., anywhere from twenty to forty or sixty pages, — an amount of reading matter that will take the average man a whole forenoon to read. I say, granted that all this vast quantity of material is harmless in itself to moral life, yet here is the reason why it seems to me Christ would, as I am doing now, advise this church and the people of Milton to avoid reading the Sunday paper, because it forces upon the thought of the community the very same things which have been crowding in upon it all the week, and in doing this necessarily distracts the man's thoughts, and makes the elevation of his spiritual nature exceedingly doubtful or difficult. I defy any preacher in this town to make much impression on the average man who has come to church saturated through and through with sixty pages of Sunday newspaper, that is, supposing the man who has read that much is in a frame of mind to go to church. But that is not the point. It is not a question of press *versus* pulpit. The press and the pulpit are units of our modern life which ought to work hand in hand. And the mere matter of church attendance might not count, if it were a question with the average man whether he would go to church and hear a dull ser-

mon or stay at home and read an interesting newspaper. That is not the point. The point is
whether the day of Rest and Worship shall be like
every other day ; whether we shall let our minds go
right on as they have been going, to the choking up
of avenues of spiritual growth and religious service.
Is it right for us to allow in Milton the occurrence
of base-ball games and Sunday racing and evening
theatres? How far is all this demoralizing to our
better life? What would Christ say, do you think?
Even supposing he would advise this church to take
and read the big Sunday paper sent in on the special
Sunday train, that keeps a small army of men at
work and away from all Sunday privileges, even supposing he would say it was all right to sell fruit and
cigars and meat on Sunday, and perfectly proper for
church-members to buy these things on that day,
what would Christ say was the real purpose of this
day in the thought of the Divine Creator when he
made the day for man?

"I cannot conceive that he would say anything
less than this to the people of this town and this
church : he would say it is our duty to make this
day different from all other days in the two particulars of Rest and Worship. He would say that we
owe it to the Father of our souls in common gratitude for his mighty love toward us that we spend
the day in ways pleasing to him. He would say
that the wonderful civilization of our time should
study how to make this day a true rest day to the
working-man of the world, and that all unnecessary

carrying of passengers or merchandise should stop, so as to give all men, if possible, every seven days, one whole day of rest and communion with something better than the things that perish with the using. He would say that the Church and the church-member and the Christian everywhere should do all in his power to make the day a glad, powerful, useful, restful, anticipated twenty-four hours, looked forward to with pleasant longing by little children and laboring men and railroad men and street-car men as the one day of all the week, happiest and best because different in its use. And so different should this day be that when Monday's toil begins the man feels refreshed in body and in soul because he has paused a little while in the mad whirl of his struggle for bread and fame, and has fellowshipped with heavenly things, and heard something diviner than the jangling discords of this narrow, selfish earth.

"If this thought of Sunday is bigotry or narrowness, then I stand convicted as a bigot living outside of the nineteenth century. But I am not concerned about that. What I am concerned about is Christ's thought of this day. If I understand his spirit right I believe he would say what I have said. He would say that it is not a right use of this day for the men and women of this generation to buy and sell merchandise, to attend or countenance places or spectacles of amusement, to engage in card parties at their homes, to fill their thoughts full of the ordinary affairs of business or the events of the world. He would say that it is the Christian's duty and privilege in this age to elevate the uses of this day so that everything done and said should tend to lift the race up higher, and make it better acquainted with the nature of God and its own eternal destiny. If Christ would not take that view of this great question, then I have totally misconceived and misunderstood his character. 'The Sabbath was made for man.' It was made for him that he might make of it a shining jewel in the string of pearls which should adorn all the days of the week, every day speaking of divine things to the man, but Sunday opening up the beauty and grandeur of the eternal life a little wider yet.

"This, dear friends all, has been my message to you this morning. May God forgive whatever has been spoken contrary to the heart and spirit of our dear Lord."

If Phillip's sermon two months before had made him enemies, this sermon made him even more. He had unconsciously this time struck two of his members very hard. One of them was part owner in a meat market which his partner kept open on Sunday. The other leased one of the parks where the base-ball games had been played. Other persons in the congregation felt more or less hurt by the plain way Phillip spoke,— especially the members who took and read the Sunday paper. They went away feeling that while much that he said was true there was too much strictness in the minister's view of the whole subject. This feeling grew as days went on. People said Phillip did not know all the facts in regard to people's business and the complications which necessitated Sunday work, and so forth.

These were the beginnings of troublous times for Phillip. The trial of the saloon-keeper was coming on in a few days and Phillip would be called to witness in the case. He dreaded it with a nervous dread peculiar to his sensitive temper. Nevertheless he went on with his church work, studying the problem of the town, endearing himself to very many in and out of his church by his manly courageous life, and feeling the heart-ache in him grow as the sin burden of the place weighed heavier on him. These were days when Phillip did much praying, and his regular preaching, which grew in power with the common people, told the story of his night vigils with the Christ he adored.

It was at this particular time that a special event occurred which put its mark on Phillip's work in Milton and became a part of its warp and woof, — a thing hard to tell, but necessary to relate as best one may.

He came home late one evening from some church meeting, letting himself into the parsonage with the night-key, and not seeing his wife in the sitting-room where she was in the habit of reading and sewing, he walked on into the small sewing room where she sometimes sat at special work, thinking to find her there. She was not there. Phillip opened the kitchen door and inquired of the servant, who sat there reading, where his wife was.

" I think she went upstairs a little while ago," was the reply.

Phillip went at once upstairs into his study and to his alarm found his wife had fainted away. She lay on the floor in front of his desk. As Phillip stooped to raise her he noticed two pieces of paper, one of them addressed to " The Preacher " and the other to " The Preacher's Wife." They were anonymous scrawls, threatening the lives of the minister and his wife. On his desk, driven deep into the wood was a large knife. Then said Phillip, with a prayer, " Verily, an enemy hath done this."

6

CHAPTER IV.

THE anonymous letters, or rather scrawls, which Phillip found by the side of his unconscious wife as he stooped to raise her up, read as follows : —

"PREACHER: Better pack up and leave. Milton is not big enough to hold you alive. Take warning in time."

"PREACHER'S WIFE: As long as you stay in Milton there is danger of two funerals. Dynamite kills women as well as men."

Phillip sat by the study lounge, holding these scrawls in his hand as his wife was recovering from her fainting fit after he had applied restoratives. His heart was filled with horror at the thought of the complete cowardice which could threaten the life of an innocent woman. There was with it all a feeling of intense contempt of such childish, dime-novel methods of intimidation as that of sticking a knife into the study desk. If it had not been for its effect on his wife, Phillip would have laughed at the whole thing. As it was, he was surprised and alarmed that she had fainted, — a thing he had never known her to do ; and as soon as she was able to speak he listened anxiously to her story.

"It must have been an hour after you had gone, Phillip, that I thought I heard a noise upstairs, and thinking perhaps you had left one of your windows down at the top and the curtain was flapping, I went right up, and the minute I stepped into the room I had the feeling that some one was there."

" Did n't you carry up a light? "

" No. The lamp was burning at the end of the upper hall and so I never thought of needing more. Well, as I moved over toward the window, still feeling that strange, unaccountable knowledge of some one there, a man stepped out from behind your desk, walked right up to me and held out those letters in one hand, while with the other he threw the light from a small bull's-eye or burglar's lantern upon them."

Phillip listened in amazement.

"Sarah, you must have dreamed all that! It is n't likely that any man would do such a thing."

" Phillip, I did not dream. I was terribly wide-awake, and so scared that I could n't even scream. My tongue seemed to be entirely useless. But I felt compelled to read what was written, and the man held the papers there until the words seemed to burn my eyes. He then walked over to the desk and with one blow drove the knife down into the wood, and then I fainted away, and that is all I can remember."

"And what became of the man?" asked Phillip, still inclined to think that his wife had in some way fallen asleep and dreamed at least a part of this strange scene, perhaps before she went up to the study and discovered the letters.

"I don't know; maybe he is here in the house yet. Oh, Phillip, I am almost dead with fear,— not for myself, but for your life!"

"I never had any fear of anonymous letters or of threats," replied Phillip, contemptuously eying the knife which was still sticking in the desk. "Evidently the saloon men think I am a child, to be frightened with these bugaboos which have figured in every cheap detective story since the time of Captain Kidd."

"Then you think this is the work of the saloon men?"

"Who else can it be? We have no other enemies of this sort in Milton."

"But they will kill you! Oh, Phillip, I cannot bear the thought of living here in this way. Let us leave this dreadful place!"

"Little woman," said Phillip, while he bravely drove away any slight anxiety he may have had for himself, "don't you think it would be cowardly to run away so soon?"

"Wouldn't it be better to run away too soon than to be killed? Is there any bravery in staying in a place where you are likely to be murdered by some coward?"

"I don't think I shall be," said Phillip, confidently. "And I don't want you to be afraid. They will not dare to harm you."

"No, Phillip!" exclaimed his wife, eagerly;

"you must not be mistaken. I did not faint away to-night because I was afraid for myself. Truly, I have no fear there. It was the thought of the peril in which you stand daily as you go out among these men, and as you go back and forth to your meetings in the dark. I am growing nervous and anxious ever since the shooting; and when I was startled by the man here to-night I was so weak that I fainted. But I am sure they do not care to harm me; you are the object of their hatred. If they strike any one it will be you. That is the reason I want you to leave this place. Say you will, Phillip. Surely there are other churches where you could preach as you desire to do and still not be in such constant danger."

It required all of Phillip's wisdom and love and discernment of his immediate duty to answer his wife's appeal and say no to it. It was one of the severest struggles he had ever had. There was to be taken into the account not only his own safety, but that of his wife as well. For, think what he would, he could not shake off the feeling that a coward so cowardly as to resort to the assassination of a man would not be over particular even if the victim should chance to be a woman. Phillip was man enough to be entirely unshaken by anonymous threats. A thousand a day would not have unnerved him in the least. He would have writhed under the sense of the great sin which they revealed, but that is all the effect they would have had.

When it came to his wife, however, that was

another question. For a moment he felt like send-
ing in his resignation and moving out of Milton as
soon as possible. But finally he decided that he
ought to remain; and Mrs. Strong did not oppose
his decision when once he had declared it. She
knew Phillip must do what to him was the will of
his Master, and with that she was content.

She had overcome her nervousness and dread
now that Phillip's courageous presence strengthened
her, and she began to tell him that he had better
hunt for the man who had appeared so mysteriously
in the study.

"I have n't convinced myself yet that there is
any man. Confess, Sarah, that you dreamed all
that."

"I did not," replied his wife, a little indignantly.
"Do you think I wrote those letters and stuck that
knife into the desk myself?"

"Of course not. But how could a man get into
the study and neither you nor the girl know it?"

"I did hear a noise, and that is what started me
upstairs. And he may be in the house yet. I shall
not rest easy until you look into all the closets and
down cellar and everywhere."

So Phillip, to quiet his wife, searched the house
thoroughly, but found nothing. The servant and the
minister's wife followed along at a respectful distance
behind Phillip, one armed with the poker and the
other with a fire-shovel, while he pulled open closet
doors with reckless disregard of any possible man
hiding within, and pretended to look into the most

unlikely places for him, joking all the while to reassure his trembling followers.

They found one of the windows in Phillip's study partly open. But that did not prove anything, although a man might have crawled in and out again through that window from a wing of the parsonage, the roof of which ran so near the window that an active person could gain entrance that way. The whole affair remained more or less a mystery to Phillip. However, the letters and the knife were real. He took them down town next day to the office of the evening paper, and asked the editor to publish the letters and describe the knife. It was too good a piece of news to omit, and Milton people were treated to a genuine sensation when the article came out. Phillip's object in giving the incident publicity was to show the community what a murderous element it was fostering in the saloon power. Those threats and the knife preached a sermon to the thoughtful people of Milton, and citizens who had never asked the question before began to ask now, "Are we to endure this saloon monster much longer?"

As for Phillip he went his way the same as ever. Some of his friends and church-members even advised him to carry a revolver and be careful about going out alone at night. Phillip laughed at the idea of a revolver and said, "If the saloon men want to get rid of me without the trouble of shooting me themselves they had better make me a present of a silver-mounted pistol; then I should manage the shooting myself. And as for being careful about going out in the evenings, what is this town thinking of, that it will continue to license and legalize an institution that makes its honest citizens advise new-comers to stay at home for fear of assassination? No. I shall go about my work just as if I lived in the most law-abiding community in America. And if I am murdered by the whiskey men I want the people of Milton to understand that the citizens will be as much to blame for the murder as the saloon men. For a community that will license such a curse ought to bear the shame of the legitimate fruits of it."

The trial of the man with the hare-lip had been postponed for some legal reason, and Phillip felt relieved somewhat. He dreaded the ordeal of the court scene. And one or two visits made to the jail had not been helpful to him. The man had refused each time to see the minister, and he had gone away feeling hungry in his soul for the man's redemption, and realizing something of the spirit of Christ when he was compelled to cry out, " Ye will not come unto me that ye might have life." That always seemed to Phillip the most awful feature of the history of Christ, — that the very people he loved and yearned after spit upon him and finally broke his heart with their hatred.

He continued his study of the problem of the town, believing that every place has certain peculiar local characteristics which every church and preacher ought to study. He was struck by the aspect of the lower part of the town, where nearly all the poorer people lived. He went down there and studied the situation thoroughly. It did not take a very great amount of thinking to convince him that the church power in Milton was not properly distributed. The seven largest churches in the place were all on one street, well up in the wealthy residence portion, and not more than two or three blocks apart. Down in the tenement district there was not a single church building, and only one or two weak mission-schools which did not touch the problem of the district at all. The distance from this poor part of the town to the churches was fully a mile, a distance that certainly stood as a geographical obstacle to the church attendance of the neighborhood, even supposing the people were eager to go to the large churches, which was not at all the fact. Indeed, Phillip soon discovered that the people were indifferent in the matter. The churches on the fashionable street in town meant less than nothing to them. They never would go to them, and there was little hope that anything the pastors or members could do would draw the people that distance to come within church influence. The fact of the matter was the seven churches of different denominations in Milton had no living connection whatever with nearly one half the population, and that the most needy half, of the place.

The longer Phillip studied the situation, the more unchristian it looked to him, and the more he longed to change it. He went over the ground again and again very carefully.   He talked with the other ministers, and the most advanced Christians in his own church.   There was a variety of opinion as to what might be done, but no one was ready for the radical move which Phillip advocated when he came to speak on the subject the first Sunday of the month.

The first Sunday was beginning to be more or less dreaded or anticipated by Calvary Church people.   They were learning to expect something radical, sweeping, almost revolutionary in Phillip's utterances on Christ and Modern Society.   Some agreed with him as far as he had gone.   Very many had been hurt at his plainness of speech.   This was especially true of the property owners and the fashionable part of Phillip's membership.   Yet there was a fascination about Phillip's preaching that prevented, so far, any very serious outbreak or dissension in the church.   Phillip was a recognized leader.   In his presentation of the truth he was large-minded.   He had the faculty of holding men's respect.   There was no mistaking the situation, however.   Mr. Winter, with others, was working against him.   Phillip was vaguely conscious of much that did not develop into open, apparent fact.   Nevertheless, when he came up on the first Sunday of the next month he found an audience that crowded the church to the doors, and in the audience were scattered numbers of men from the working-men's district with whom Phillip had talked while down there.   It was, as before, an inspiring congregation, and Phillip faced it feeling sure in his heart that he had a great subject to unfold, and a message to deliver to the Church of Christ such as he could not but believe Christ would most certainly present if he were visibly present in Milton.

He began by describing the exact condition of affairs in Milton. To assist this description he had brought with him into the church his map of the town.

"Look now," he said, pointing out the different localities, "at B. Street where we now are. Here are seven of the largest churches of the place on this street. The entire distance between the first of these church buildings and the last one is a little over half a mile. Three of these churches are only two blocks apart. Then consider the character of the residences and people in the vicinity of this street. It is what is called desirable; that is, the homes are the very finest, and the people almost without exception are refined, respectable, well-educated, and Christian in training. All the wealth of the town centres about B. Street. All the society life extends out from it on each side. It is considered the most fashionable street for drives and promenades. It is well-lighted, well-paved, well-kept. The people who come out of the houses on B. Street are always well dressed and comfortable looking. Mind you," continued Phillip, raising his hand with a significant gesture, "I do not want to have you think that I consider good clothes and comfortable looks as unchristian or anything against

the people who present such an appearance. Far
from it. I simply mention this fact to make the
contrast I am now going to show you all the plainer.
For let us leave B. Street now and go down into the
flats by the river where nearly all the mill people
have their homes. I wish you would note first the
distance from B. Street and the churches to this
tenement district. It is nine blocks, — that is, a
little over a mile. To the edge of the tenement
houses farthest from our own church building it is a
mile and three quarters. And within that entire district, measuring nearly two by three miles, there is
not a church building. There are two feeble mission-schools, which are held in plain, unattractive
halls, where every Sunday a handful of children meet;
but nothing practically is being done by the Church
of Christ in this place to give the people in that
part of the town the privileges and power of the life
of Christ, the life more abundantly. The houses
down there are of the cheapest description. The
people who come out of them are far from well-
dressed. The streets and alleys are dirty and ill-
smelling. And no one cares to promenade for
pleasure up and down the sidewalks in that neighborhood. It is not a safe place to go to alone at
night. The most frequent disturbances come from
that part of the town. All the hard characters find
refuge there. And let me say that I am not now
speaking of the working people. They are almost
without exception law-abiding. But in every town
like ours the floating population of vice and crime

seeks naturally that part of a town where the poorest houses are, and the most saloons, and the greatest darkness both physical and moral.

" If there is a part of this town which needs to be lifted up and cleaned and healed and inspired by the presence of the Church of Christ it is right there where there is no church. The people on B. Street and for six or eight blocks each side know the gospel. They have large numbers of books and papers and much Christian literature. They have been taught Bible truths; they are familiar with them. Of what value then is it to continue to support on this short street, so near together, seven churches of as many different denominations which have for their members the respectable, moral people of the town? I do not mean to say that the well-to-do, respectable people do not need the influence of the Church and the preaching of the gospel. But they can get these privileges without such a fearful waste of material and power. If we had only three or four churches on this street they would be enough. We are wasting our strength with the present arrangement. We are giving the rich and the educated and well-to-do people seven times as much church as we are giving the poor, the ignorant, and the struggling workers in the tenement district. There is no question, there can be no question, that all this is wrong. It is opposed to every principle that Christ advocated. And in the face of these plain facts which no one can dispute there is a duty before these churches on this street which cannot be denied without denying the very purpose of a church. It is that duty which I am now going to urge upon this Calvary Church.

"It has been said by some of the ministers and members of the churches that we might combine in an effort and build a large and commodious mission in the tenement district. But that, to my mind, would not settle the problem at all, as it should be settled. It is an easy and a lazy thing for church-members to put their hands in their pockets and say to a few other church-members, 'We will help build a mission, if you will run it after it is up; we will attend our church up-town here, while the mission is worked for the poor people down there.' That is not what will meet the needs of the situation. What that part of Milton needs is the Church of Christ in its members, — the whole Church, on the largest possible scale. What I am now going to propose, therefore, is something which I believe Christ would advocate, if not in the exact manner I shall explain, at least in the same spirit."

Phillip paused a moment and looked out over the congregation earnestly. The expectation of the people was roused almost to the point of a sensation as he went on.

"I have consulted with competent authorities, and they say that our church building here could be moved from its present foundation without serious damage to the structure. A part of it would have to be torn down to assist the moving, but it could easily be replaced. The expense would not be more than we could readily meet. We are out of debt, and the property is free from incumbrance. What I propose, therefore, is a very simple thing, — that we move our church edifice down into the heart of the tenement district, where we can buy a suitable lot for a comparatively small sum, and at once begin the work of a Christian church in the very neighbor-hood where such work is most needed.

"There are certain objections to this plan. I think they can be met by the exercise of the Christ spirit of sacrifice and love. A great many members will not be able to go that distance to attend service, any more than the people there at present can well come up here. But there are six churches left on B. Street. What is to hinder any Christian member of Calvary Church from working and holding fel-lowship with those churches, if he cannot put in his service in the tenement district? None of those churches are crowded ; they will welcome the advent of more members. But the main strength of the plan which I propose lies in the fact that if it be done, it will be a live illustration of the eagerness of the Church to reach and save men. The very sight of our church moving down off this street to the lower part of the town will be an object lesson to the people ; and the Church will at once begin to mean something to them. Once established there, we can work from it as a centre. The distance ought to be no discouragement to any healthy per-son. There is not a young woman in this church that is in the habit of dancing who does not make twice as many steps during an evening dancing party as would be necessary to take her to the tenement district and back again. Surely any Christian church-member is as willing to endure fatigue, and sacrifice as much time to help to make men and women better, as he is to have a good time himself. Think for a moment what this move which I propose would mean to the life of this town, and to our own Christian growth ! At present we go to church and listen to a good choir, we listen to preaching, we go home again, we have a pleasant Sunday-school, we are all comfortable and well clothed here and enjoy our services, we are not disturbed by the sight of disagreeable or uncongenial people. But is that Christianity? Where do the service and the self-denial and the working for men's souls come in? Ah, my dear brothers and sisters, what is this church really doing for the salvation of men in this place? Is it Christianity merely to have a comfortable church and go to it once or twice a week to enjoy nice music and listen to preaching, and then go home to a good dinner? What have we sacrificed? What have we denied ourselves? What have we done to show the poor or the sinful that we care anything for their souls, or that Christianity is anything but a comfortable, select religion for those who can afford the good things of the world? What has the church in Milton done to make the workingman here feel that it is an institution that throbs with the brotherhood of man? And what do we know as a church of the problems that face the tenement-dwellers and the wage-earners? But suppose we actually move our church down there and then go there ourselves week-days and Sundays to work for the uplifting of immortal beings. Shall we not then have the satisfaction of knowing that we are at least trying to do something more than enjoy our church all by ourselves? Shall we not be able to hope that we have at least attempted to obey the spirit of our sacrificing Lord, who commanded his disciples to go and make disciples of the nations? It seems to me that the plan I propose is a Christian plan. If the churches in this neighborhood were not so numerous, if the circumstances were different, it might not be wise or necessary to do what I propose. But as the facts are, I solemnly believe that this church has an opportunity before it to show Milton and the other churches and the world that it is willing to do an unusual thing if it has within it the spirit of complete willingness to reach and lift up mankind in the way that will do it best and most speedily. If individuals are commanded to sacrifice and endure for Christ's sake and kingdom, I do not know why organizations should not do the same. And in this instance something on a large scale, something that represents large sacrifice, something that will convince the people of the love of man for man, is the only thing that will strike deep enough into the problem of the tenement district in Milton to begin to solve it in any satisfactory or Christian way.

" I do not expect the church to act on my plan without due deliberation.   I have arrived at my own conclusions after carefully going over the entire ground.   And in the sight of all the need and degradation of the people and in the light of all that Christ has made clear to be our duty as his disciples, there is but one path open to us.   If we neglect to follow him as he beckons us, I believe we shall neglect the one opportunity of Calvary Church to put itself in the position of the true Church of the crucified Lamb of God, who did not please himself, who came to minister to others, who would certainly approve of any steps his Church on earth in this age might honestly take to reach men and love them and become to them the helper and savior and life-giver which the great Head of the Church truly intended we should be.   I leave this plan which I have proposed before you, for your Christian thought and prayer.   And may the Holy Spirit guide us all into all the truth.   Amen."

If Phillip had deliberately planned to create a sensation, he could not have done anything more radical to bring it about   If he had stood on the platform and fired a gun into the audience it would not have startled the members of Calvary Church more than this calm proposal to them that they move their church building a mile away from its aristocratic surroundings.   Nothing that he had said in his previous sermons had provoked such a spirit of opposition.   This time the church was roused.   Feelings of astonishment, indignation, and alarm agitated the members of Calvary Church. Some of them gathered about Phillip at the close of the service.

" It will not be possible to do this thing you propose, Brother Strong," said one of the deacons, a leading member and a man who had defended Phillip once or twice against public criticism.

" Why not? " asked Phillip, simply. He was exhausted with his effort that morning, but felt that a crisis of some sort had been precipitated by his message, and so he welcomed this show of interest which his sermon had aroused.

" The church will not agree to such a thing."

" A number of them favor the step," replied Phillip, who had talked over the matter fully with many in the church.

" A majority will vote against it."

" Yes, an overwhelming majority ! " said one man. " I know a good many who would not be able to go that distance to attend church, and they certainly would not join any other church on the street. I know for one *I* would n't."

" Not if you thought Christ's kingdom in this town would be advanced by it?" asked Phillip, turning to this man with a directness that was almost bluntness.

" I don't see how that would be a test of my Christianity."

" That is not the question," said one of the trustees, who had the reputation of being a very shrewd business man. " The question is concerning the feasibility of moving this property a mile into the poorest part of the town and then maintaining it there. In my opinion it cannot be done. The expenses of the organization cannot be kept up. We should lose some of our best financial supporters. Mr. Strong's spirit and purpose spring from a good motive, no doubt, but viewed from a business point of view the church in that locality would not be a success. To my mind it would be a very unwise thing to do. It would practically destroy our organization here and not really establish anything there."

" I do not believe we can tell until we try," said Phillip. " I certainly do not wish the church to destroy itself foolishly. But I do feel that we ought to do something very positive and very large to define our attitude as saviors to this community. And moving the building as I propose has the advantage of being a definite practical step in the direction of a Christlike use of our powers .as a church."

There was more talk of the same sort but it was plainly felt by Phillip that the plan he had proposed was distasteful to the greater part of the congregation, and if the matter came to a vote it would be defeated. He talked the plan over with his trustees as he had already done before he spoke in public. Four of them were decided in their objection to the plan. Only one fully sustained Phillip. During the week he succeeded in finding out that from his membership of five hundred, less than forty persons

were willing to stand by him in so radical a movement. And yet the more Phillip studied the problem of the town, the more he was persuaded that
the only way for the church to make any impression on the tenement district was to put itself
directly in touch with the neighborhood. To accomplish that necessity Phillip was not stubborn.
He was ready to adopt any plan that would actually
do something, but every day that he spent in his
study of the town he grew more eager to have the
church feel its opportunity and make Christ a
reality to those most in need of him.

It was at this time that Phillip was surprised one
evening by a call from one of the working-men
who had been present and heard his sermon on
moving the church into the tenement district.

"I came to see you particularly, Mr. Strong,
about getting you to come down to our hall some
evening next week and give us a talk on some
subject connected with the signs of the times."

"I'll come if you think I can do any good that
way," replied Phillip, hesitating a little.

"I believe you can. The men are beginning
to take to you, and while they won't come up to
church they will turn out to hear you down there."

"All right. When do you want me to come?"

"Say next Tuesday. You know where the
hall is?"

Phillip nodded. He had been by it in his walks
through that part of Milton.

The spokesman for the workmen expressed his

thanks and arose to go, but Phillip asked him to stay a few moments. He wanted to know at first hand what the workingmen would do if the church should at any time decide to act after Phillip's plan.

"Well, to tell the truth, Mr. Strong, I don't believe very many of them would join any church."

"That is not the question. Would they feel the church any more there than where it is now?"

"Yes, I honestly think they would. They would come out to hear you."

"Well, that would be something, to be sure," replied Phillip, smiling. "But as to the wisdom of my plan, — how does it strike you on the whole?"

"I would like to see it done. I don't believe I shall, though."

"Why?"

"Your church won't agree to it."

"Maybe they will in time."

"I hope they will. And yet let me tell you, Mr. Strong, even if you succeeded in getting your church and people to come into the tenement district you would find plenty of people there who would n't go near you."

"I suppose that is so. But oh, that we might do something!" Phillip clasped his hands over his knee and gazed earnestly at the man opposite. The man returned the gaze almost as earnestly. It was the impersonation of the Church confronting the laboring man, each in a certain way asking the other, "What will the Church do?" And it was a noticeable fact that the minister's look revealed more doubt and anxiety than the other man's look, which contained more or less of indifference and distrust. Phillip sighed, and his visitor soon after took his leave.

So it came about that Phillip Strong plunged into a work which from the time he stepped into the dingy little hall and faced the crowd peculiar to it had a growing influence on all his strange career, which rapidly grew in strangeness as days came on.

He was invited again and again to address the men in that part of Milton. They were almost all mill-employees. They had a simple organization for debate and discussion of questions of the day. Gradually the crowds increased as Phillip continued to come, and developed a series of talks on Christian Socialism. There was standing room only. He was beginning to know a number of the men and a strong affection was growing up in their hearts for him.

That was just before the time the trouble at the mills broke out. He had just come back from the hall where he had now been going every Tuesday evening, and where he had spoken on his favorite theme, "the meaning and responsibility of power, both financial and moral." He had treated the subject from the Christian point of view entirely. He had several times roused his rude audience to enthusiasm. Moved by his theme and his surroundings he had denounced, with even more than usual vigor, those men of ease and wealth who did nothing with their money to help their brothers.

He had mentioned, as he went along, what great responsibility any great power puts on a man, and had dealt in a broad way with the whole subject of power in men as a thing to be used, and always used for the common good.

He did not recall his exact statements, but felt a little uneasy as he walked home, for fear he might possibly have influenced his particular audience against the rich as a class. He had not intended anything of the kind, but had a vague idea that possibly he ought to have guarded some words or sentences more carefully.

He had gone up into his study to finish some work, when the bell rang sharply, and he came down to open the door just as Mrs. Strong came in from the other room, where she had been giving directions to the girl, who had gone upstairs through the kitchen.

The minister and his wife opened the door together, and one of the neighbors rushed into the hall so excited he could hardly speak.

" Oh, Mr. Strong, won't you go right down to Mr. Winter's house at once? You have more influence with those men than any one around here ! "

"What men?"

" The men who are going to kill him if some one does n't stop it ! "

"What ! " cried Phillip, turning pale, not from fear, but from self-reproach to think he might have made a mistake. " Who is trying to kill him, — the mill-men?"

"Yes! No! I do not, cannot tell. But he is in great danger, and you are the only man in this town who can help to save him. Come!"

Phillip turned to his wife. "Sarah, it is my duty. If anything should happen to me you know my soul will meet yours at the gates of Paradise."

He kissed her, and rushed out into the night.

CHAPTER V

WHEN Phillip reached the residence of Mr. Winter he found himself at once in the midst of a mob of howling angry men who surged over the lawn and tramped the light snow that was falling into a muddy mass over the walks and up the veranda steps. A large electric lamp out in the street in front of the house threw a light over the strange scene.

Phillip wedged his way in among the men, crying out his name, and asking for room to be made so that he could see Mr. Winter. The crowd, under the impulse which sometimes moves excited bodies of men, yielded to his request. There were cries of, "Let him have a minister if he wants one!" "Room here for the priest!" "Give the preacher a chance to do some praying where it's needed mighty bad!" and so on. Phillip found a way opened for him as he struggled toward the house, and he hurried forward fearing some great trouble, but hardly prepared for what he saw when he reached the steps of the veranda.

Half a dozen men had the mill-owner in their grasp, having evidently just dragged him out of his dining-room. His coat was half torn off, as if there had been a struggle. Marks of bloody fingers

stained his collar. His face was white, and his eyes
filled with the fear of death. Within, upon the
floor, lay his wife, who had fainted. A son and a
daughter, his two grown-up children clung terrified
to one of the servants, who kneeled half fainting herself by the side of the mill-owner's wife. A table
overturned and fragments of a late dinner scattered over the floor, a broken plate, the print of a
muddy foot on the white tiling before the open fire,—
the whole picture flashed upon Phillip like a scene
out of the French Revolution, and he almost rubbed
his eyes to know if he was awake and in America
in the nineteenth century. He was intensely practical, however, and the nature of his duty never for
a moment escaped him. He at once advanced and
said calmly : —

"What does all this mean? Why this attack on
Mr. Winter?"

The moment Mr. Winter saw Phillip and heard
his voice he cried out, trembling : "Is that you,
Mr. Strong? Thank God ! Save me ! Save me !
They are going to kill me !"

"Who talks of killing, or taking human life contrary to law !" exclaimed Phillip, coming up close
and placing his hand on Mr. Winter's arm. "Men,
what are you doing?"

For a moment the crowd fell back a little from
the mill-owner, and one of the men who had been
foremost in the attack replied with some respect,
although in a sullen manner, "Mr. Strong, this is
not a case for your interference. This man has

caused the death of one of his employees and he deserves hanging."

"And hanging he will get!" yelled another. A great cry arose. In the midst of it all Mr. Winter shrieked out his innocence. "It is all a mistake! They do not know! Mr. Strong, tell them they do not know!"

The crowd closed around Mr. Winter again. Phillip knew enough about men to know that the mill-owner was in genuine danger. Most of his assailents were the foreign element in the mills. Many of them were under the influence of liquor. The situation was critical. Mr. Winter clung to Phillip with the frantic clutch of a man who sees only one way of escape, and clings to that with mad eagerness. Phillip turned around and faced the mob. He raised his voice, hoping to gain a hearing and reason with it. But he might as well have raised his voice against a tornado. Some one threw a handful of mud and snow toward the prisoner. In an instant every hand reached for the nearest missile, and a shower of stones, muddy snow-balls, and limbs torn from the trees on the lawn, was rained upon the house. Most of the windows in the lower story were broken. All this time Phillip was eagerly remonstrating with the few men who had their hands on the mill-owner. He thought if he could only plead with them to let Mr. Winter go he could slip with him around the end of the veranda through a side door and take him through the house to a place of safety. He also knew that every minute was precious, as the police might arrive at any moment and change the situation.

But in spite of his pleas the mill-owner was gradually pushed and dragged down off the veranda toward the gate. The men tried to get Phillip out of the way.

"We don't want to harm you, sir. Better get out of danger," said the same man who had spoken before.

Phillip for answer threw one arm about Mr. Winter, saying, "If you kill him, you will kill me with him. You shall never do this great sin against an innocent man. In the name of God I call on every soul here to —"

But his words were drowned in the noise that followed. The mob was insane with fury. Twice Mr. Winter was dragged off his feet by those down on the walk. Twice Phillip raised him to his feet, feeling sure that if the crowd once threw him down they would trample him to death. Once some one threw a rope over the wretched man's head. Phillip snatched it off again. Both he and Mr. Winter were struck again and again. Their clothes were torn into tatters. Mr. Winter was faint and reeling. Only his great terror made his clutch on Phillip like that of a drowning man.

At last the crowd had dragged the two outside the gate into the street. Here they paused awhile and Phillip again spoke to the mob: —

"Men, made in God's image, listen to me! Do not take innocent life. If you kill him, you kill me

also.   For I will never leave his side alive, and I
will not permit such murder if I can prevent it."

" Kill them both,— the bloody coward and the
priest ! " yelled a voice.   " They both belong to the
same church."

" Yes, hang 'em ! hang 'em both ! "   A tempest
of cries went up.   Phillip towered up like a giant.
In the light of the street lamp he looked out over
the great sea of passionate, brutal faces crazed with
drink and riot, and a great wave of compassionate
feeling swept over him.   It was Christlike in its
yearning love for lost children.   His lips moved in
prayer.

And just then the outer circle of the crowd
seemed agitated.   It had surged up nearer the light
with the evident intention of hanging the mill-owner
on one of the cross pieces of a telegraph pole near
by.   The rope had again been thrown over his head.
Phillip stood with one arm about Mr. Winter, and
with the other hand stretched out in entreaty, when
he heard a pistol-shot, then another.   The entire
police department had been summoned, and had
now arrived.   There was a skirmishing rattle of
shots.   But the crowd began to scatter in the neighborhood of the police force.   Then those nearer
Phillip began to run as best they could away from
the officers.   Phillip and the mill-owner were
dragged along with the rest in the growing confusion, until, watching his opportunity, Phillip pulled
Mr. Winter behind one of the large poles by which
the lights of the street were suspended.

Here, sheltered but struck by many a blow, Phillip managed to shield with his own body the man who only a little while before had come into his own house and called him a liar and threatened to withdraw his church support, because of the preaching of Christ's principles.

When finally the officers reached the two men Mr. Winter was nearly dead from the fright. Phillip was badly bruised, but not seriously, and he helped Mr. Winter back to the house. A few of the police remained on guard the rest of the night. It was while recovering from the effects of the night's attack that Phillip little by little learned of the facts that led up to the assault.

There had been a growing feeling of discontent in all the mills, and it had finally taken shape in the Ocean Mill, which was largely owned and controlled by Mr. Winter. The discontent arose from a new scale of wages submitted by the company. It was not satisfactory to the men, and the afternoon of that evening on which Phillip had gone down to the hall, a committee of the mill men had gone away without getting any satisfaction. They could not agree on the proposition made by the company and by their own labor organization. Later in the day one of the committee, under instructions, went to see Mr. Winter alone, and came away from the interview very much excited and angry. He spent the first part of the evening in a saloon, where he related a part of his interview with the mill-owner, and said that he had finally kicked him out of the office.

Still later in the evening he told several of the men that he was going to see Mr. Winter again, knowing that on certain evenings he was in the habit of staying down at the mill office until nearly half-past nine for special business. The mills were undergoing repairs, and Mr. Winter was away from home more than usual.

That was the last that any one saw of the man until, about ten o'clock, some one going home past the mill office heard a man groaning at the foot of a new excavation at the end of the building, and climbing down discovered the man who had been to see Mr. Winter twice that afternoon. He had a terrible gash in his head and lived only a few minutes after he was discovered. To the half-dozen men who stood over him in the saloon near by, where he had been carried, he had murmured the name of "Mr. Winter," and had then expired.

A very little enrages men already heated with rum and hatred. The rumor spread like lightning that the wealthy mill-owner had killed one of the employees who had gone to see him peaceably to arrange matters for the men. He had thrown him out of the office into one of the new mill excavations and left him there to rot like a dog in a ditch. So the story ran all through the tenement district, and in an incredibly short time the worst elements in Milton were surging toward the mill-owner's house with murder in their hearts, and the means of accomplishing it in their hands.

Mr. Winter had finished his work at the office

and gone home to sit down to a late lunch, as his custom was, when he was interrupted by the mob. The rest of the incident is connected with what has been told. The crowd seized him with little ceremony, and it was only Phillip's timely arrival and his occupying the interval until the police arrived that prevented a lynching in Milton that night. As it was, Mr. Winter received a scare from which it took a long time to recover. He dreaded to go out alone at night. He kept on guard a special watchman, and lived in more or less terror even then. It was satisfactorily proved in a few days that the man who had gone to see Mr. Winter had never reached the office door. But coming around the corner of the building where the new work was being done, he had fallen off the stone work, striking on a rock in such a way as to produce a fatal wound. This tempered the feeling of the workmen toward Mr. Winter; but unrest and discontent had seized on every man employed in the mills, and as the winter drew on, affairs reached a crisis.

The difference between the mills and the men over the scale of wages could not be settled. The men began to talk about a strike. Phillip heard of it, and at once, with his usual frankness and boldness, spoke with downright plainness to the men. That was at the little hall a week after the attempt on Mr. Winter's life. Phillip's part in that night's event had added to his reputation and his popularity with the men. They admired his courage and his grit. Most of them were ashamed of the whole

8

affair, especially after they had sobered down and it had been proved that Mr. Winter had not touched the man. So Phillip was welcomed with applause as he came out on the little platform and looked over the crowded room, seeing many faces there that had glared at him in the mob a week before. And yet his heart told him he loved these men, and his reason told him that it was the sinner and the unconverted that God loved. It was a terrible responsibility to have such men count him popular, and he prayed that wisdom might be given him in the approaching crisis, especially as he seemed to have some real influence.

He had not spoken ten words when some one cried, "Come outside ! Big crowd out here want to get in." It was moonlight and not very cold, so every one moved out of the hall, and Phillip mounted the steps of a storehouse near by and spoke to a crowd that filled up the street in front and for a long distance right and left. His speech was very brief, but it was fortified with telling figures, and at the close he stood and answered a perfect torrent of questions. His main counsel was against a strike in the present situation. He had made himself famil- iar with the facts on both sides. Strikes, he argued, except in very rare cases, were demoralizing, — an unhealthy, disastrous method of getting justice done. "Why, just look at that strike in Preston, England, among the cotton spinners. There were only 660 operatives, but that strike before it ended threw out of employment over 7,800 weavers and other workmen who had nothing whatever to do with the quarrel of the 660 men. In the recent strike in the cotton trade in Lancashire, at the end of the first twelve weeks the operatives had lost in wages alone $4,500,000. Four strikes that occurred in England between 1870 and 1880 involved a loss in wages of more than $25,000,000. In 2,200 strikes investigated lately by the National Bureau of Labor, it is estimated that the employees lost about $51,800,000, while the employers lost only $30,700,000. Out of 351 strikes in England between 1870 and 1880, 191 were lost by the strikers, 71 were gained, and 91 compromised ; but in the strikes that were successful, it took several years to regain in wages the amount lost by the enforced idleness of the men."

There were enough hard-thinking sensible men in Phillip's audience that night to see the force of his argument. The majority, however, were in favor of a general strike to gain their point in regard to the scale of wages. When Phillip went home he carried with him the conviction that a general strike in the mills was pending. In spite of the fact that it was the worst possible season of the year for such action, and in spite of the fact that the difference demanded by the men was a trifle compared with their loss of wages the very first day of idleness, there was a determination among the leaders that the fifteen thousand men in the mills should all go out in the course of a few days if the demands of the men in the Ocean Mill were not granted.

What was the surprise of every one in Milton,

therefore, the very next day when it was announced that every mill in the great system had shut down, and not a man of the fifteen thousand laborers who marched to the buildings in the early gray of the winter morning found entrance. Statements were posted up on the doors that the mills were shut down until further notice. The mill-owners had stolen, a march on the employees, and the big strike was on; but it had been started by Capital, not by Labor, and Labor went to its tenement or congregated in the saloon, sullen and gloomy; and, as days went by and the mills showed no signs of opening, the great army of the unemployed walked the streets of Milton in growing discontent and fast accumulating debt and poverty.

Meanwhile the trial of the man arrested for shooting Phillip came on, and Phillip and his wife both appeared as witnesses in the case. The man was convicted, and sentenced to fifteen years' imprisonment. It has nothing special to do with the history of Phillip Strong, but may be of interest to the reader to know that in two years' time he was pardoned out and returned to Milton to open his old saloon, where he actually told more than once the story of his attempt on the preacher's life.

There came on also during those stormy times in Milton the trial of several of the men arrested for the assault on Mr. Winter. Phillip was also summoned as a witness in these cases. As always, he frankly testified to what he knew and saw. Several of the accused were convicted, and sentenced to short terms. But the mill-owner, probably fearful of revenge on the part of the men, did not push the matter, and most of the cases went by default for lack of prosecution.

Mr. Winter's manner toward Phillip underwent a change after that memorable evening when the minister stood by him at the peril of his own life. There was a feeling of genuine respect mingled with fear in the mill-owner's deportment toward Phillip. To say that they were warm friends would be saying too much. Men as widely different as the minister and the wealthy mill-man do not come together on that sacred ground of friendship, even where one is indebted to the other for his life. A man may save another from hanging and still be unable to save him from selfishness. And the mill-owner went his way and Phillip went his, on a different basis so far as common greeting went, but no nearer in that oneness of aim in life which makes heart-to-heart communion possible. For the time being, Mr. Winter's hostility was submerged under his indebtedness to Phillip. He returned to his own place in the church and contributed to the financial support.

One day at the close of a month, Phillip came into the cosey parsonage, and, instead of going right up to his study as his habit was when his outside work was done for the day, he threw himself down on a couch by the open fire. His wife was at work in the other room, but she came in, and, seeing Phillip lying there, inquired what was the matter.

"Nothing, Sarah, with me. Only I'm sick at heart with the sight and knowledge of all this wicked town's sin and misery."

"Do *you* have to carry it all on your shoulders, Phillip?"

"Yes," replied Phillip, almost fiercely. It was not that either. Only, his reply was like a great sob of conviction that he must bear something of the town's burden. He could not help it.

Mrs. Strong did not say anything for a moment. Then, —

"Don't you think you take it too seriously, Phillip?"

"What?"

"Other people's wrong-doing. You are not responsible."

"Am I not? I am my brother's keeper. What quantity of guilt may I not carry into the eternal kingdom if I do not do what I can to save him! Oh, how can men be so selfish? Yet I am only one person. I cannot prevent all this suffering alone."

"Of course you can't, Phillip. You wrong yourself to take yourself to task so severely for the sins of others. But what has stirred you up so at this time?" Mrs. Strong understood Phillip well enough to know that some particular case had roused his feeling. He seldom yielded to such despondency without some immediate practical reason.

Phillip sat up on the couch and clasped his hands over his knee with the eager earnestness that characterized him when he was roused.

"Sarah, this town slumbers on the smoking crest of a volcano. There are more than fifteen thousand people here in Milton out of work. A great many of them are honest, temperate people who have saved up a little. But it is nearly gone. The mills are shut down, and, on the authority of men who ought to know, shut down for all winter. The same condition of affairs is true in a greater or less degree in the entire State and throughout the country and even the world. People are suffering to-day in this town for food and clothing and fuel through no fault of their own. The same thing is true of thousands and even hundreds of thousands all over the world. It is an age that calls for heroes, martyrs, servants, saviors. And right here in this town, where distress walks the streets and actual want already has its clutch on many a poor devil, society goes on giving its expensive parties and living in its little round of selfish pleasure just as if the volcano were a downy little bed of roses for it to go to sleep on whenever it wearies of the pleasure and wishes to retire to happy dreams. Oh, but the bubble will burst one of these days, and then — "

Phillip swept his hand upward with a fine gesture, and sunk back upon the couch, groaning.

"Don't you exaggerate?" The minister's wife put the question gently.

"Not a bit! Not a bit! All true. I am not one of the French Revolution fellows, always lugging in blood and destruction, and prophesying calamity to the nation and the world if it does n't gee and

haw the way *I* tell it to.   But I tell you, Sarah, it
takes no prophet to see that a man who is hungry
and out of work is a dangerous man to have around.
And it takes no very extraordinary-sized heart to
throb a little with righteous wrath when in such
times as these people go right on with their useless
luxuries of living, and spend as much in a single
evening's entertainment as would provide a comfortable living for a whole month to some deserving
family."

" How do you know they do ? "

" Well, I 'll tell you.   I 've figured it out.   I will
leave it to any one of good judgment that any one
of these projected parties mentioned here in the
evening paper," Phillip smoothed the paper out on
the head of the couch, — " any one of them will cost
in the neighborhood of one hundred to one hundred and fifty dollars.   Look here !   Here's the
Goldens' party, — members of Calvary Church.
They will spend at least twenty-five or thirty dollars
for flowers ; and refreshments will cost fifty more ;
and   music another twenty-five ; and incidentals
twenty-five   extra, — and   so   on.   Is   that   right,
Sarah, in these times, and as people ought to live
now ? "

" But some one gets the benefit of all this money
spent.   Surely that is help to some of the working-
people."

" Yes, but how many people are helped by such
expenditures?   Only a select few, and they are the
very ones who are least in need of it.   I say the

Christian people and members of churches have no
right, under the conditions that face us as a town
and a nation and a world, I say they have no right
to indulge their selfish pleasures to this extent in
these ways. I know that Christ would not approve
of it."

"You think he would not, Phillip."

"No, I *know* he would not. There is not a particle of doubt in my mind about it. What right has
a disciple of Jesus Christ to spend for the gratifica-
tion of his physical or æsthetic pleasures money
which ought to be feeding the hungry bodies of
men or providing some useful necessary labor for
their activity? — I mean of course those pleasures
that a man can live without. In this age of the
world society ought to dispense with some of its
accustomed pleasures and deny itself for the sake
of the great suffering, needy world. Instead of that,
the members of the very Church of Christ on earth
spend more in a single evening's entertainment for
people who don't need it than they give to the salvation of men in a whole year. I protest out of the soul
God gave me against such wicked selfishness. And
I will protest though society spurn me from it as a
bigot, a puritan, and a boor. For society in Christian America is not Christian in this matter, — no,
not after the Christianity of Christ!"

"What can you do about it, Phillip?" His wife
asked the question sadly. She had grown old fast
since coming to Milton. And a presentiment of
evil would, in spite of her naturally cheery disposi-

tion, cling to her whenever she considered Phillip and his work.

"I can preach on it, and I will."

"Be wise, Phillip. You tread on difficult ground when you enter society's realm."

"Well, dear, I will be as wise as a serpent and harmless as a dove, although I must confess I never knew just exactly how much that verse meant. But preach on it I must and will."

And when the first Sunday of the month came, Phillip did preach on it, to the dismay of several members of his church who were in the habit of giving entertainments and card-parties on a somewhat elaborate scale.

He had never preached on the subject of amusements, and he stated that he wished it to be plainly understood that he was not preaching on the subject now. It was a question which went deeper than that, and took hold of the very first principles of social science. A single passage in the sermon will show the drift of it all.

"We have reached a time in the history of the world when it is the Christian duty of every man who calls himself a disciple of the Master to live on a simpler, less extravagant basis. The world has been living beyond its means. Modern civilization has been exorbitant in its demands. And every dollar foolishly spent to-day means suffering for some one who ought to be relieved by that money wisely expended. An entertainment given by people of means to other people of means in these hard times, in which money is lavished on flowers, delicacies, and dress, is in my opinion an act of which Christ could not approve. I do not mean to say that he would object to the pleasure which flowers, delicacies, and dress will give. But he would say that it is an unnecessary enjoyment and expense at this particular crisis through which we are passing. He would say that money and time should be given where people more in need of them might have the benefit. He would say that when a town is in the situation of ours to-day it is not a time for the selfish use of any material blessing. Unless I mistake the spirit of the modern Christ, if he were here to-day he would preach to the whole world the necessity of a far simpler, less expensive style of living, and, above all, actual self-denial on the part of society for the Brotherhood of man. What is society doing now? What sacrifices is it making? When it gives a charity ball, does it not spend twice as much in getting up the entertainment to please itself as it makes for the poor in whose behalf the ball is given? Do you think I am severe? Ask yourself, O member of Calvary Church, what has been the extent of your sacrifice for the world this year before you condemn me for being too strict or particular. It is because we live in such times that the law of service presses upon us with greater insistence than ever. And now more than during any of the ages gone, Christ's words ring in our ears with twenty centuries of reverberation, 'Whosoever will not deny himself and take up his cross, he cannot be my disciple.' "

Of all the sermons on Christ and Modern Society which Phillip had thus far preached, none had hit so hard or been applied so personally as this. The Goldens went home from the service in a towering rage. "That settles Calvary Church for me," said Mrs. Golden, as she flung herself out of the building after the service was over. " I consider that the most insulting sermon I ever heard from any minister. It is simply outlandish ; and how the church can endure such preaching much longer is a wonder to me. I don't go near it again while Mr. Strong is the minister!" Phillip did not know it yet, but he was destined to find out that society carries a tremendous power in its use of the word "outlandish," applied either to persons or things.

When the evening service was over, Phillip, as his habit was, lay down on the couch in front of the open fire until the day's excitement had subsided a little. It was almost the only evening in the week when he gave himself up to complete rest of mind and body.

He had been lying there about a quarter of an hour when Mrs. Strong, who had been moving the plants back from one of the front windows and had been obliged to raise a curtain, stepped back into the room with an exclamation.

" Phillip! There is some one walking back and forth in front of the house! I have heard the steps ever since we came home. And just now I saw a man stop and look in here. Who can it be ? "

"Maybe it's the man with the burglar's lantern come back to get his knife," said Phillip, who had always made a little fun of that incident as his wife had told it. However, he rose and went over to the window. Sure enough, there was a man out on the sidewalk looking straight at the house. He was standing perfectly still.

Phillip and his wife stood by the window looking at the figure outside, and, as it did not move away, at last Phillip grew a little impatient and went to the door to open it and ask the man what he meant by staring into people's houses that fashion.

"Now, Phillip, do be careful, won't you?" entreated his wife, anxiously.

"Yes, I presume it is some tramp or other wanting food. There's no danger, I know."

Phillip flung the door wide open and called out in his clear, hearty voice : —

"Anything you want, man? Come up and ring the bell if you want to get in and know us, instead of standing there on the walk catching cold and making us wonder who you are."

In response to this frank and informal invitation the figure came forward and slowly mounted the steps of the porch. As the face came into view more clearly, Phillip started and fell back a little.

It was not because the face was that of an enemy, or because it was repulsive, or because he recognized an old acquaintance. It was a face he had never to his knowledge seen before. Yet the impulse to start back before it seemed to spring from the recollec-

tion of just such a countenance moving over his
spirit when he was in prayer or in trouble. It all
passed in a second's time and then he confronted
the man as a complete stranger.

There was nothing remarkable about him. He
was poorly dressed and carried a small bundle.
He looked cold and tired. Phillip, who never could
resist the mute appeal of distress in any form,
reached out his hand and said kindly, " Come, my
brother, you look cold and weary. Come in and
sit down before the fire, and we 'll have a bite of
lunch. I was just beginning to think of having
something to eat, myself."

Phillip's wife looked a little remonstrance, but
Phillip did not see it, and wheeling an easy chair
before the fire he made the man sit down, and pulling up a rocker he placed himself near him.

The stranger seemed a little surprised at the
action of Phillip, but made no resistance. He took
off his hat and disclosed a head of hair white as
snow, and said, in a voice that sounded singularly
sweet and true : —

"You do me much honor, sir. The fire feels
good this chilly evening, and the food will be very
acceptable. And I have no doubt you have a good
warm bed that I could occupy for the night."

Phillip stared hard at his unexpected guest, and
his wife who had started out of the room to get the
lunch, shook her head vigorously as she stood behind the visitor, as a sign that Phillip should refuse
such a strange request. Phillip was taken aback a

little, and he looked puzzled. The words were uttered in the utmost simplicity.

"Why, yes, we can arrange that all right," he said. "There is a spare room, and — excuse me a moment while I go and help to get our lunch." Phillip's wife was telegraphing to him to come into the other room and he obediently got up and went.

"Now, Phillip," whispered his wife when they were out in the dining-room, "You know that is a risky thing to do. You are all the time inviting all kinds of characters in here. We can't keep this man all night. Who ever heard of such a thing as a perfect stranger coming out with a request like that? I believe the man is crazy. It certainly will not do to let him stay here all night."

Phillip looked puzzled.

"I declare it is strange! He does n't appear like an ordinary tramp. But somehow I don't think he 's crazy. Why should n't we let him have the bed in the room off the east parlor. I can light the fire in the stove there and make him comfortable."

"But we don't know who he is. Phillip, you let your sympathies run away with your judgment."

"Well, little woman, let me go in and talk with him a while. You get the lunch, and we 'll see about the rest afterward."

So Phillip went back and sat down again. He was hardly seated when his visitor said : —

"If your wife objects to my staying here to-night

of course I don't wish to. I don't feel comfortable to remain where I'm not welcome."

"Oh, you're perfectly welcome," said Phillip, hastily, with some embarrassment, while his strange visitor went on : —

"I'm not crazy, only a little odd, you know. Perfectly harmless. It will be perfectly safe for you to keep me over night."

The man spread his white hands out before the fire, while Phillip sat and watched him with a certain fascination new to his interest in all sorts and conditions of men.

Mrs. Strong brought in a substantial lunch of cold meat, bread and butter, milk and fruit, and at Phillip's request placed it on a table in front of the open fire, where he and his remarkable guest ate like hungry men.

It was after this lunch had been eaten and the table removed that a scene occurred which would be incredible if its reality and truthfulness did not compel us to record it as a part of the life of Phillip Strong. No one will wish to deny the power and significance of this event as it is unfolded in the movement of this story.

CHAPTER VI.

" I HEARD your sermon this morning," said Phillip's guest, while Mrs. Strong was removing the table to the dining-room.

" Did you? " asked Phillip, because he could not think of anything wiser to say.

" Yes," said the strange visitor, simply. He was so silent after saying this one word that Phillip did what he was not in the habit of doing. He always shrank back sensitively from asking for an opinion of his preaching from any one except his wife. But now he could not help saying, —

" What did you think of it? "

" It was one of the best sermons I ever heard. But somehow it did not sound sincere."

" What ! " exclaimed Phillip, almost angrily. If there was one thing he felt sure about, it was the sincerity of his preaching. Then he checked his feeling, as he thought how foolish it would be to get angry at a passing tramp, who was probably a little out of his mind. Yet the man's remark had a strange power to Phillip. He tried to shake it off as he looked harder at him. The man looked over at Phillip and repeated gravely, shaking his head, " Not sincere."

Mrs. Strong came back into the room, and Phillip motioned her to sit down near him while

9

he said, "And what makes you think I was not sincere?"

"You said the age in which we lived demanded that people live in a far simpler, less extravagant style."

"Yes, that is what I said. I believe it, too," replied Phillip, clasping his hands over his knee and gazing at his singular guest with earnestness. The man's thick white hair glistened in the open firelight like spun glass.

"And you said that Christ would not approve of people spending money for flowers, food, and dress on those who did not need it, when it could more wisely be expended for the benefit of those who were in want."

"Yes; those were not my exact words, but that was my idea."

"Your idea. Just so. And yet we have had here in this little lunch, or, as you called it, a 'bite of something,' three different kinds of meat, two kinds of bread, hothouse grapes, and the richest kind of milk."

The man said all this in the quietest, most calm manner possible; and Phillip stared at him, more assured than ever that he was a little crazy. Mrs. Strong looked amused, and said, "You seemed to enjoy the lunch pretty well." The man had eaten with a zest that was redeemed from greediness only by a delicacy of manner that no tramp ever possessed.

"My dear madam," said the man, "perhaps this

was a case where the food was given to one who stood really in need of it."

Phillip started as if he had suddenly caught a meaning from the man's words he had not before heard in them.

"Do you think it was an extravagant lunch, then?" he asked with a very slight laugh.

The man looked straight at Phillip, and replied slowly, "Yes, for the times in which we live!"

A sudden silence fell on that group of three in the parlor of the parsonage, lighted up by the soft glow of the coal fire. No one except a person thoroughly familiar with the real character of Phillip Strong could have told why that silence fell on him instead of a careless laugh at the crazy remark of a half-witted stranger tramp. Just how long the silence lasted, Phillip did not know. Only, when it was broken he found himself saying, —

"Man, who are you? Where are you from? And what is your name?"

His guest turned his head a little, and replied, "When you called me in here you stretched out your hand and called me 'Brother.' Just now you called me by the great term, 'Man.' These are my names; you may call me 'Brother Man.'"

"Well, then, 'Brother Man,'" said Phillip, smiling a little to think of the very strangeness of the whole affair, "your reason for thinking I was not sincere in my sermon this morning was because of the extravagant lunch this evening?"

"Not altogether. There are other reasons." The

man suddenly bowed his head between his hands, and Phillip's wife whispered to him, " Phillip, what is the use of talking with a crazy man? You are tired, and it is time to put out the lights and go to bed. Get him out of the house now as soon as you can."

The stranger raised his head and went on talking just as if he had not broken off abruptly.

" Other reasons. In your sermon you tell people they ought to live less luxuriously. You point them to the situation in this town, where thousands of men are out of work. You call attention to the great poverty and distress all over the world, and you say the times demand that people live far simpler, less extravagant lives. And yet here you live yourself like a prince. Like a prince," he repeated, after a peculiar gesture, which seemed to include not only what was in the room but all that was in the house.

Phillip glanced at his wife as people do when they suspect a third person being out of his mind, and saw that her expression was very much like his own feeling, though not exactly. Then they both glanced around the room.

It certainly did look luxurious, even if not princely. The parsonage was an old mansion which had once belonged to a wealthy but eccentric sea-captain. He had built to please himself, something after the colonial fashion ; and large square rooms, generous fireplaces with quaint mantels, and tiling, and hard-wood floors gave the house an appearance of solid comfort that

approached luxury. The church in Milton had pur-
chased the property from the heirs, who had become involved in ruinous speculation and parted
with the house for a sum little representing its
real worth. It had been changed a little, and
modernized with new heating apparatus, although
the old fireplaces still remained ; and one spare
room, an annex to the house proper, had been
added recently. There was an air of decided
comfort bordering on luxury in the different pieces
of furniture and the whole furnishing of the room.

"You understand," said Phillip, as his glance
travelled back to his visitor, "that this house is not
mine. It belongs to my church. It is the parsonage, and I am simply living in it as the minister."

"Yes, I understand. You, a minister, and living
in this princely house while other people have not
where to lay their heads."

Again Phillip felt the same temptation to anger
steal into him, and again he checked himself at the
thought : "The man is certainly insane. The whole
thing is simply absurd. I will get rid of him. And
yet —"

He could not shake off a strange and powerful
impression which the stranger's words had made
upon him. Crazy or not, he had hinted at the
possibility of an insincerity on Phillip's part, which
made him restless. Phillip determined to question
him and see if he really would develop a streak of
insanity that would justify him in getting rid of him
for the night.

"Brother Man," he said, using the term his guest had given him, "do you think I am living too extravagantly?"

"Yes, in these times and after such a sermon."

"What would you have me do?" Phillip asked the question half seriously, half amused at himself for asking advice from such a source.

"Do as you preach others ought to."

Again that silence fell over the room. And again Phillip felt the same impression of power in the strange man's words.

The "Brother Man," as he wished to be called, bowed his head between his hands again; and Mrs. Strong whispered to Phillip: "Now it is certainly worse than foolish to keep this up any longer. The man is evidently insane. We cannot keep him here all night. He will certainly do something terrible. Get rid of him, Phillip. This may be a trick on the part of the whiskey men."

Never in all his life had Phillip been so puzzled to know what to do with a human being. Here was one, the strangest he had ever met, who had come into his house; it is true he had been invited, but once within he had invited himself to stay all night, and then had accused his entertainer of living too extravagantly and called him an insincere preacher. Add to all this the singular fact that he had declared his name to be "Brother Man," and that he spoke with a calmness that was the very incarnation of peace, and Phillip's wonder reached its limit.

In response to his wife's appeal Phillip rose abruptly and went to the front door; he opened it, and a whirl of snow danced in. The wind had changed, and the moan of a coming heavy storm was in the air.

The moment that Phillip opened the door his strange guest also rose, and putting on his hat he said, as he moved slowly towards the hall, "I must be going. I thank you for your hospitality, madam."

Phillip stood holding the door partly open. He was perplexed to know just what to do or say.

"Where will you stay to-night? Where is your home?"

"My home is with my friends," replied the man. He laid his hand on the door, opened it, and had made one step out on the porch, when Phillip, seized with an impulse, laid his hand on his arm, gently but strongly pulled him back into the hall, shut the door, and placed his back against it.

"You cannot go out into this storm until I know whether you have a place to go to for the night."

The man hesitated curiously, shuffled his feet on the mat, put his hand up to his face, and passed it across his eyes with a gesture of great weariness. There was a look of loneliness and of unknown sorrow about his whole figure that touched Phillip's keenly sensitive spirit irresistibly. If the man was a little out of his right mind, he was probably harmless. They could not turn him out into the night if he had nowhere to go.

"Brother Man," said Phillip, gently, "would you like to stay here to-night? Have you anywhere else to stay?"

"You are afraid I will do harm. But no. See. Let us sit down."

He laid his hat on the table.resumed his seat and asked Phillip for a Bible. Phillip handed him one. He opened it and read a chapter from the Prophet Isaiah, and then, sitting in the chair, bowing his head between his hands, he offered a prayer of such wonderful beauty and spiritual refinement of expression that Phillip and his wife listened with awed astonishment.

When he had uttered the amen Mrs. Strong whispered to Phillip, "Surely we cannot shut him out into the storm. We will give him the spare room."

Phillip said not a word. He at once built up a fire in the room and in a few moments invited the man into it.

"Brother Man," he said simply, "stay here as if this were your own house. You are welcome for the night."

"Yes, heartily welcome," said Phillip's wife, as if to make amends for any doubts she had felt before.

For reply the "Brother Man" raised his hand almost as if in benediction. And they left him to his rest.

In the morning Phillip knocked at his guest's door to waken him for breakfast. Not a sound could be heard within. He waited a little while and then knocked again. It was as still as before. He opened the door softly and looked in.

To his amazement there was no one there. The bed was made up neatly, everything in the room was in its place, but the strange being who had called himself " Brother Man " was gone.

Phillip exclaimed, and his wife came in.

" So our queer guest has flown ! He must have been very still about it ; I heard no noise. Where do you suppose he is? And who do you suppose he is? "

" Are you sure there ever was such a person, Phillip? Don't you think you dreamed all that about the 'Brother Man'?" Mrs. Strong had not quite forgiven Phillip for his sceptical questioning of the reality of the man with the lantern who had driven the knife into the desk.

" Yes, it 's your turn now, Sarah. Well, if our Brother Man was a dream he was the most curious dream this family ever had. And if he was crazy he was the most remarkable insane person I ever saw."

" Of course he was crazy. All that he said about our living so extravagantly proves it."

" Do you think he was crazy in that particular? " asked Phillip, in a strange voice. His wife noticed it at the time but its true significance did not become real to her until afterwards. He went to the front door and found it was unlocked. Evidently the guest had gone out that way. The heavy storm of the night had covered up any possible signs of footsteps. It was still snowing furiously.

Phillip went into his study for the forenoon as usual, but he did very little writing.   His wife could hear him pacing the floor restlessly.

About ten o'clock he came downstairs and declared his intention of going out into the storm to see if he could n't settle down to work better.

He went out and did not return until the middle of the afternoon.   Mrs. Strong was a little alarmed.

" Where have you been all this time, Phillip ? — in this terrible storm too !   You are a monument of snow.   Stand out here in the kitchen while I sweep it off you."

Phillip obediently stood still while his wife walked around him with a broom, and he good-naturedly submitted to being swept down "as if I were being worked into shape for a snow man," he said.

" Where have you been ?   Give an account of yourself."

" I have been seeing how some other people live. Sarah, the Brother Man was not so very crazy, after all.   He has more than half converted me."

" Did you find out anything about him ? "

" Yes, several of the older citizens here recognized my description of him.   They say he is harmless and has quite a history ; was once a wealthy mill-owner in Clinton.   He wanders about the country, living with any one who will take him in. It is a queer case ; I must find out more about him.   But I 'm hungry ; can I have a bite of something ? "

" Have n't you had dinner ? "

" No ; I got interested and did n't stop."

" Where have you been ? "

" Among the tenements."

" How are the people getting on there ? "

" I cannot tell. It almost chokes me to think of it."

" Now, Phillip, what makes you take it so seriously? How can you help all that suffering? You are not to blame for it ? "

" Maybe I am for a part of it. But whether I am or not, there the suffering is. And I don't know that we ought to ask who is to blame in such cases. At any rate, supposing the fathers and mothers in the tenements are themselves to blame for their own wretchedness this fearful day, having brought it all on themselves by their own sinfulness, does that make innocent children and helpless babes any warmer and better clothed and fed? Sarah, I have seen things in four hours' time that make me want to join the bomb-throwers of Europe almost."

Mrs. Strong came up behind Phillip's chair as he sat at the table eating, and placed her hand on his brow. She grew more anxious every day over his growing personal feeling for others. It seemed to her it was becoming a passion with him, wearing him out, and she feared its results as winter deepened and the lock-out in the mills remained unbroken.

" You cannot do more than one man, Phillip," she said with a sigh.

" No, but if I can only make the church see its duty at this time and act the Christlike way a great many persons will be saved. Sarah ! " He dropped his knife and fork, wheeled around abruptly in his chair, and faced her with the question, "Would you give up this home and be content to live in a simpler fashion than we have been used to since we came here?"

"Yes," replied his wife, quietly, "I will go anywhere and suffer anything with you, Phillip. What is it you are thinking of now?"

"I need a little more time. There is a crisis near at hand in my thought of what Christ would require of me. My dear, I am sure we shall be led by the spirit of Truth to do what is necessary and for the better saving of men."

He kissed his wife tenderly and went upstairs to his work. All through the rest of the afternoon and in the evening, as he shaped his church and pulpit work, the words of the "Brother Man" rang in his ears, and the situation at the tenements rose in the successive pictures of a panorama before his eyes. As the storm increased in fury with the coming darkness, Phillip felt that it was typical in a certain sense of his own condition. He abandoned the work he had been doing at his desk and kneeling down at his couch prayed. Mrs. Strong, coming up to the study to see how his work was getting on, found him kneeling there and went and kneeled beside him while together they sought the light through the storm.

So the weeks went by and the first Sunday of the next month found Phillip's Christ message even more direct and personal than any he had brought to his people before. He had spent much of the time going into the working-men's homes. The tenement district was becoming familiar territory to him now. He had settled finally what his own action ought to be. In that action his wife fully concurred. And the members of Calvary Church coming in that Sunday morning were astonished at the message of their pastor as he spoke to them from the standpoint of the modern Christ.

" I said a month ago that the age in which we live demands a simpler, less extravagant style of living. I did not mean by that to condemn the beauties of art or the marvels of science or the products of civilization. I merely emphasized what I believe is a mighty but neglected truth in our modern civilization, — that if we would win men to Christ we must adopt more of his spirit of simple and consecrated self-denial. I wish it to be distinctly understood as I go on that I do not condemn any man because he is rich or lives in a luxurious house, enjoying every comfort of modern civilization and every delicacy of the season. What I do wish distinctly understood is the belief which has been burned deep into me ever since coming to this town, that if the members of this church wish to honor the Head of the Church and bring men to believe him and be saved in this life and the next they must be willing to do far more than they have yet done to make use of the physical comforts and luxuries of their homes for the blessing and Christianizing of this community. In this particular I have myself failed to set you an example. The fact that I have so failed is my only reason for making this matter public this morning.

"The situation in Milton to-day is exceedingly serious. I do not need to prove it to you by figures. If any business man will go through the tenements he will acknowledge my statements. If any woman now in this house will contrast those dens with her own home, she will, if Christ is a power in her heart, stand in horror before such a travesty of the ideal happy home of the working-man. The destitution of the neighborhood is alarming. The number of men out of work is dangerous. The complete removal of all sympathy between the Church up here on this street, and the tenement district is sadder than death. O my beloved!"—Phillip stretched out his arms and uttered a cry that rang in the ears of those who heard it and remained with some of them a memory for years,—"these things ought not so to be! Where is the Christ spirit with us! Have we not sat in our comfortable houses and eaten our pleasant food and dressed in the finest clothing and gone to amusements and entertainments without number, while God's poor have shivered on the streets, and his sinful ones have sneered at Christianity as they walked by our church doors?

"It is true we have given money to charitable causes. It is true the town council has organized a bureau for the care and maintenance of those in want. It is true members of Calvary Church

with other churches at this time have done something to relieve the immediate distress of the town.
But how much have we given of ourselves to those
in need? Do we reflect that to reach souls and
win them, to bring back humanity to God and the
Christ, the Christian must do something different
from the giving of money now and then? He
must give a part of himself. That was my reason
for urging you to move this church building away
from this street into the tenement district, that we
might give ourselves to the people there. The
idea is the same in what I now propose. But
you will pardon me if first of all I announce my own
action, which I believe is demanded by the times
and would be approved by our Lord."

Phillip stepped up near the front of the platform
and spoke with an earnestness and power which
thrilled every hearer. A part of the great conflict
through which he had gone that past month shone
out in his pale face and found partial utterance in
his impassioned speech, especially as he drew near
the end. The very abruptness of his proposition
smote the people into breathless attention.

"The parsonage in which I am now living is a
large, even a luxurious dwelling. It has nine large
rooms. You are familiar with its furnishing. The
salary this church pays me is two thousand dollars,
a sum which more than provides for my necessities.
What I have decided to do is this : I wish this church
to reduce this salary one half and apply the other
thousand dollars to the fitting up of the parsonage,

as a refuge for homeless children, or for some such purpose which may commend itself to your best judgment. There is money enough in this church alone to maintain such an institution handsomely, and not a single member of Calvary suffer any hardship whatever. I will move into a house nearer the lower part of the town, where I can more easily reach after the people and live more among them. That is what I propose for myself. It is not because I believe the rich and the educated do not need the gospel or the church. The rich and the poor both need the life more abundantly. But I am firmly convinced that as matters now are, the church-membership through pulpit and pew must give itself more than in the later ages of the world it has done for the sake of winning men. The form of our own self-denial must take a definite, physical, genuinely sacrificing shape. The Church must get back to the apostolic times in some particulars and an adaptation of community of goods and a sharing of certain aspects of civilization must mark the church-membership of the coming twentieth century. An object lesson in self-denial large enough for men to see, a self-denial that actually gives up luxuries, money, and even harmless pleasures, — this is the only kind that will make much impression on the people. I believe if Christ were on earth he would again call for this expression of loyalty to him. He would again say, 'So likewise whosoever he be of you that forsaketh not all that he hath, he cannot be my disciple?'

" All this is what I call on the members of this
church to do. Do I say that you ought to abandon
your own houses and live somewhere else? No. I
can decide only for myself in a matter of that kind.
But this much I do say. Give yourselves in some
genuine way to save this town from its wretchedness.
It is not so much your money as your own soul that
the sickness of the world demands. This plan has
occurred to me. Why could not every family in this
church become a savior to some other family that
is actually in need of saving. Let the church family
interest itself in the other, know the extent of its
wants as far as possible, go to it in person, let the
Christian home come into actual touch with the
unchristian, in short, become a natural savior to
one family. There are dozens of families in this
church that could do that. It would take money.
It would take time. It would mean real self-denial.
It would call for all your Christian grace and courage. But what does all this church-membership and
church life mean if not just such sacrifice? We
cannot give anything to this age of more value than
our own selves. The world of sin and want and
despair and disbelief is not hungering for money or
mission-schools or charity balls or state institutions
for the relief of distress, but for live, pulsing, loving
Christian men and women, who reach out live, warm
hands, who are willing to go and give themselves,
who will abandon, if necessary, if Christ calls for it,
the luxuries they have these many years enjoyed in
order that the bewildered, disheartened, discontented,

unhappy, sinful creatures of earth may actually learn of the love of God through the love of man. And that is the only way the world ever has learned of the love of God. Humanity brought that love to the heart of the race, and it will continue so to do until this earth's tragedy is all played and the last light put out. Members of Calvary Church, I call on you in Christ's name this day to do something for your Master that will really be a self-denial for you. Consider the age in which you live. And give yourselves to it in a way that will make men believe beyond a doubt that you really mean what you say when you claim to be a disciple of that One who, although rich, yet for our sakes became poor, giving up all heaven's glory in exchange for all earth's misery, the end of which was a cruel and bloody crucifixion. Are we Christ's disciples unless we follow him in this particular? We are not our own. We are bought with a price."

When that Sunday morning service closed, Calvary Church was stirred to its depths. There were more excited people talking together all over the church than Phillip had ever seen before. He greeted several strangers as usual and was talking with one of them, when one of the trustees came up and said the Board would like to meet with Phillip if convenient for him as soon as he was at liberty.

Phillip accordingly waited in one of the Sunday-school class-rooms with the trustees, who had met immediately after the sermon, and decided to have an instant conference with the pastor.

CHAPTER VII.

THE door of the class-room was closed and Phillip and the trustees were together. There was a moment of embarrassing silence and then the spokesman for the Board, a nervous little man, said : —

"Mr. Strong, we hardly know just what to say to this proposition of yours this morning about going out of the parsonage and turning it into an orphan asylum. But it is certainly a very remarkable proposition and we felt as if we ought to meet you at once and talk it over."

"It's simply impossible," spoke up one of the trustees. "In the first place it is impracticable as a business proposition."

"Do you think so?" asked Phillip, quietly.

"It is out of the question!" said the first speaker, excitedly. "The church will never listen to it in the world. For my part, if Brother Strong wishes to — "

At that moment the sexton knocked at the door and said a man was outside very anxious to see the minister and have him come down to his house. There had been an accident, or a fight, or something. Some one was dying and wanted Mr. Strong at once. So Phillip hastily excused himself and went out, leaving the trustees together.

The door was hardly shut again when the speaker who had been interrupted jumped to his feet and exclaimed : —

"As I was saying, for my part, if Brother Strong wishes to indulge in this eccentric action he will not have the sanction of my vote in the matter! It certainly is an entirely unheard-of and uncalled-for proposition."

"Mr. Strong has, no doubt, a generous motive in this proposed action," said the third member of the Board; "but the church will most certainly oppose any such step as the giving up of the parsonage. He exaggerates the need of such a sacrifice. I think we ought to reason him out of the idea."

"We called Mr. Strong to the pastorate of Calvary Church," said another; "and it seems to me he came under the conditions granted in our call. For the church to allow such an absurd thing as the giving up of the parsonage to this proposed outside work would be a very unwise move."

"Yes, and more than that," said the first speaker, "I want to say very frankly that I am growing tired of the way things have gone since Mr. Strong came to us. What business has Calvary Church with all these outside matters, these labor troubles and un-employed men and all the other matters that have been made the subject of preaching lately? I want a minister who looks after his own parish. Mr. Strong does not call on his own people; he has

not been inside my house but once since he came
to Milton. Brethren, there is a growing feeling of
discontent over this matter."

There was a short pause and then one of the
members said : —

" Surely if Mr. Strong feels dissatisfied with his
surroundings in the parsonage or feels as if his work
lay in another direction, he is at liberty to choose
another parish. But he is the finest pulpit-minister
we ever had, and no one doubts his entire sincerity.
He is a remarkable man in many respects."

" Yes, but sincerity may be a very awkward thing
if carried too far. And in this matter of the parsonage I don't see how the trustees can allow it.
Why, what would the other churches think of it ?
Calvary Church cannot allow anything of the kind,
for the sake of its reputation. But I would like to
hear Mr. Winter's opinion; he has not spoken
yet."

The rest turned to the mill-owner, who as chairman of the Board usually had much to say, and was
regarded as a shrewd and careful business adviser.
In the excitement of the occasion and discussion
the usual formalities of a regular Board-meeting had
been ignored.

Mr. Winter was evidently embarrassed. He had
listened to the discussion of the minister with his
head bent down and his thoughts in a whirl of
emotion both for and against the pastor. His
naturally inclined business habits contended against
the proposition to give up the parsonage; his

feelings of gratitude to the minister for his personal help the night of the attack by the mob rose up to defend him.   There was with it all an under-current of self-administered rebuke that the pastor had set the whole church an example of unselfishness.   He wondered how many of the members would voluntarily give up half their incomes for the good of humanity.   He wondered in a confused way how much he would give up himself.   Phillip's sermon had made a real impression on him.

"There is one point we have not discussed yet," he said at last.   "And that is Mr. Strong's offer of half his salary to carry on the work of a children's refuge or something of that kind."

"How can we accept such an offer?   Calvary Church has always believed in paying its minister a good salary, and paying it promptly; and we want our minister to live decently and be able to appear as he should among the best people," replied the nervous little man who had been first to speak.

"Still, we cannot deny that it is a very generous thing for Mr. Strong to do.   He certainly is entitled to credit for his unselfish proposal; no one can charge him with being worldly-minded," said Mr. Winter, feeling a new interest in the subject as he found himself defending the minister.

"Are you in favor of allowing him to do what he proposes in the matter of the parsonage?" asked another.

"I don't see that we can hinder Mr. Strong

from living anywhere he pleases. The church cannot compel him to live in the parsonage."

" No, but it can choose not to have such a minister !" exclaimed the first speaker again, excitedly ;
" and I for one am most decidedly opposed to the
whole thing. I do not see how the church can
allow it and maintain its self-respect."

" Do you think the church is ready to tell Mr.
Strong that his services are not wanted any longer ? "
asked Mr. Winter coldly.

" I am, for one of the members, and I know
others who feel as I do if matters go on this way
much longer. I tell you, Brother Winter, Calvary
Church is very near a crisis. Look at the Goldens
and the Malverns and the Albergs. They are all
leaving us ; and the plain reason is the nature of
the preaching. Why, you know yourself, Brother
Winter, never has the pulpit of Calvary Church
heard such preaching on people's private affairs."

Mr. Winter colored up and replied angrily, " What
has that to do with the present matter? If the
minister wants to live in a simpler style I don't see
what business we have to try to stop it. As to the
disposition of the parsonage, that is a matter or
business which rests with the church to arrange."

The nervous, irritable little man who had spoken
oftenest rose to his feet and exclaimed, " You can
count me out of all this, then ! I wash my hands
of the whole affair ! " and he went out of the room,
leaving the rest of the Board somewhat surprised
and confused by his sudden departure.

They remained about a quarter of an hour longer, discussing the matter, and finally, at Mr. Winter's suggestion, a committee was appointed to confer with the minister the next evening and see if he could not be persuaded to modify or change his proposition made in the morning sermon. The rest of the trustees insisted that Mr. Winter himself should act as chairman of the committee, and after some remonstrance he with great reluctance agreed to do so.

So Phillip next evening, as he sat in his study mapping out the week's work and wondering a little what the church would do in the face of his proposal, received the committee, welcoming them in his bright, hearty manner. He had been notified on Sunday evening of the approaching conference. The committee consisted of Mr. Winter and two other members of the Board.

Mr. Winter opened the conversation with considerable embarrassment and an evident repugnance to his share in the matter.

"Mr. Strong, we have come, as you are aware, to talk over your proposition of yesterday morning concerning the parsonage. It was a great surprise to us all."

Phillip smiled a little. "Mrs. Strong says I act too much on impulse, and do not prepare people enough for my statements. But one of the greatest men I ever knew used to say that impulse was a good thing to obey instantly if there was no doubt of its being a right one."

"And do you consider this proposed move of yours a right one, Mr. Strong?" asked Mr. Winter.

"I do," replied Phillip, with quiet emphasis. "I do not regret making it, and I believe it is my duty to abide by my original decision."

"Do you mean that you intend actually to move out of this parsonage?" asked one of the other members of the committee.

"Yes." Phillip said it so quietly and yet so decidedly that the committee was silent a moment. Then Mr. Winter said : —

"Mr. Strong, this matter is likely to cause trouble in the church, and we might as well understand it frankly. The trustees believe that as the parsonage belongs to the church property, and was built for the minister, he ought to live in it. The church will not understand your desire to move out."

"Do you understand it, Mr. Winter?" Phillip put the question point-blank.

"No, I don't know that I do, wholly." Mr. Winter colored and replied in a hesitating manner.

"I gave my reasons yesterday morning. I do not know that I can make them plainer. The truth is I cannot go on preaching to my people about living on a simpler basis while I continue to live in surroundings that on the face of them contradict my own convictions. In other words, I am living beyond my necessities here. I have lived all my life surrounded by the luxuries of civilization. If now I desire to give the benefit of them to those who have never enjoyed them, or to know from closer contact something of the bitter struggle of the poor, why should I be hindered from putting that desire into practical form?"

"The question is, Mr. Strong," said one of the other trustees, "whether this is the best way to get at it. We do not question your sincerity nor doubt your honesty; but will your leaving the parsonage and living in a less expensive house on half your present salary help your church work or reach more people and save more souls?"

"I am glad you put it that way," exclaimed Phillip, eagerly turning to the speaker. "That is just it. Will my proposed move result in bringing the church and the minister into closer and more vital relations with the people most in need of spiritual and physical uplifting? Out of the depths of my nature I believe it will. The chasm between the Church and the people in these days must be bridged by the spirit of sacrifice in material things. It is in vain for us to preach spiritual truths unless we live physical truths. What the world is looking for to-day is object lessons in self-denial on the part of Christian people."

For a moment no one spoke. Then Mr. Winter said : —

"About your proposal that this house be turned into a refuge or home for homeless children, Mr. Strong, do you consider that idea practicable? Is it business? Is it possible?"

"I believe it is, very decidedly. The number of

homeless and vagrant children at present in Milton
would astonish you. This house could be put into
beautiful shape as a detention house until homes
could be found for the children in Christian
families."

"It would take a great deal of money to manage
it."

"Yes," replied Phillip, with a sadness which had
its cause deep within him, "it would cost something. But can the world be saved cheaply? Does
not every soul saved cost an immense sum, if not of
money at least of an equivalent? Is it possible for us
to get at the heart of the great social problem without feeling the need of using all our powers to solve
it rightly?"

Mr. Winter shook his head. He did not understand the minister. His action and his words were
both foreign to the mill-owner's regular business
habits of thought and performance.

"What will you do, Mr. Strong, if the church
refuses to listen to this proposed plan of yours?"

"I suppose," answered Phillip, after a little pause,
"the church will not object to my living in another
house at my own charges?"

"They have no right to compel you to live
here." Mr. Winter turned to the other members
of the committee. "I said so at our previous
meeting. Gentlemen, am I not right in that?"

"It is not a question of our compelling Mr.
Strong to live here," said one of the others. "It is
a question of the church's expecting him to do so.

It is the parsonage and the church home for the minister. In my opinion there will be trouble if Mr. Strong moves out. People will not understand it."

"That is my feeling, too, Mr. Strong," said Mr. Winter. "It would be better for you to modify or change, or better still, to abandon this plan. It will not be understood and will cause trouble."

"Suppose the church should rent the parsonage to some party, then," suggested Phillip; "it would then be getting a revenue from the property. That, with the thousand dollars on my salary, could be wisely and generously used to relieve much suffering in Milton this winter. The church could easily rent the house."

That was true, as the parsonage stood on one of the most desirable parts of B. Street and would command good rental.

"Then you persist in this plan of yours, do you, Mr. Strong?" asked the third member of the committee, who had for the most part been silent.

"Yes, I consider that under the circumstances, local and universal, it is my duty. Where I propose to go there is a house which I can get for eight dollars a month. It is near the tenement district, and not so far from the church and this neighborhood that I need be isolated too much from my church family."

Mr. Winter looked serious and perplexed. The other trustees looked dissatisfied. It was evident they regarded the whole thing with disfavor.

Mr. Winter rose abruptly. He could not avoid a feeling of anger, in spite of his obligation to the minister. He also had a vivid recollection of his former interview with the pastor in that study. And yet the mill-owner struggled with vague resistance against a feeling that Phillip was proposing to do a thing that could result for himself in only one way, — in suffering. With all the rest went a suppressed but conscious emotion of wonder that a man would of his own free will give up a luxurious home for the sake of anybody.

"The matter of reduction of salary, Mr. Strong, will have to come before the church. The trustees cannot vote to accept your proposal. I am very much mistaken if the members of Calvary Church will not oppose the reduction. You can see how it would place us in an unfavorable light."

"Not necessarily, Mr. Winter," said Phillip, eagerly. "If the church will simply regard it as my own great desire and as one of the ways by which we may help forward our work in Milton, I am very sure we need have no fear of being put in a false light. The church does not propose this reduction. The proposal comes from me, and in a time of peculiar emergency both financial and social. It is a thing which has been done several times before by other ministers."

"That may be. Still, I am positive that Calvary Church will regard it as unnecessary and will oppose it."

"It will not make any difference, practically," replied Phillip, with a smile. "I can easily dispose of a thousand dollars where it is needed by others more than by me. But I would prefer that the church would actually pay out the money to them, rather than myself."

Mr. Winter and the other trustees looked at Phillip in wonder; and with a few words of farewell they left the parsonage.

The following week Calvary Church held a meeting. It was one of the stormiest meetings ever held by the members. In that meeting Mr. Winter again, to the surprise of nearly all, advised caution, and defended the minister's action up to a certain point. The result was a condition of waiting and expectancy, rather than downright condemnation of the proposed action on Phillip's part. It would be presenting the church in a false light to picture it as entirely opposed, up to this date, to Phillip's preaching and ideas of Christian living. He had built up a strong buttress of admiring and believing members in the church. This stood, with Mr. Winter's influence, as a breakwater against the tidal wave of opposition beginning to pour in upon him. There was an element in Calvary Church conservative to a degree, and yet strong in its growing belief that Christian action and Church work in the world had reached a certain crisis, which would result either in the death or the life of the Church in America. Phillip's preaching had strengthened that feeling. His last move had startled the thoughtful element, and it wished to wait for developments. The proposal of some that the minister be requested to resign was finally overruled, and it was decided not to oppose his desertion of the parsonage, while the matter of reduction of salary was voted upon in the negative.

But feeling was roused to a high pitch. Many of the members declared their intention of refusing to attend services. Some declared they would not pay their pledges any longer. A small majority, however, ruled in favor of Phillip, and the action of the meeting was formally sent him by the clerk.

Meanwhile Phillip moved out of the parsonage into his new quarters. The daily paper, which had given a sensational account of his sermon, laying most stress upon his voluntary proposition referring to his salary, now came out with a column and a half devoted to Phillip's carrying out of his determination to abandon the parsonage and get nearer the people in the tenements. The article was widely copied and variously commented upon. In Milton, Phillip's action was condemned by many, defended by some. Very few seemed to understand his exact motive. The majority took it as an eccentric move, and expressed regret in one form and another that a man of such marked intellectual power as Mr. Strong seemed to possess lacked balance and good judgment. Some called him a crank. The people in the tenement district were too much absorbed in their sufferings and selfishness to make any demonstration. It remained to be seen whether they would be any better touched by Phillip in his new home.

So matters stood when the first Sunday of a new

month came, and Phillip again stood before his church with his Christ message. It had been a wearing month to him. Gradually there had been growing upon him a sense of almost isolation in his pulpit work. He wondered if he had inter-preted the Christ aright. He studied with re-newed earnestness the springs of action that moved the historical Jesus, and again and again put that resplendently calm, majestic, suffering personality into his own pulpit in Milton, and then stood off, as it were, to watch what he would, in all human prob-ability, say. He reviewed all his own sayings on those first Sundays and tried to tax himself with utmost severity for any denial of his Master or any false presentation of his spirit; and as he went over the ground he was almost overwhelmed to think how little had been really accomplished. This time he came before the church with the experience of nearly three weeks' hand-to-hand work among the people for whose sake he had moved out of the parsonage. As usual an immense congregation thronged the church.

"The question 'What is church work?' has come to me lately in different forms," began Phillip. "I am aware that my attitude on this question is not shared by many of the members of this church and other churches. Nevertheless, I stand here to-day, as I have stood on these Sundays, to declare to you what in deepest humility would seem to me to be the attitude of Christ in the matter before us.

"What is a church? It is a body of disciples

professing to acknowledge Christ as Master. What does he want such a body to be? Like himself in spirit, in daily life. What does he want such a body to do? Whatever will most effectively make God's kingdom come on earth, and his will be done as in heaven. What is the most necessary work of this church in Milton? It is to go out and seek and save the lost. It is to take up its cross and follow the Master. And as I see him to-day he beckons this church to follow him into the tenements and slums of this town and be Christs to those who do not know him. As I see him he stands beckoning with pierced palms in the direction of suffering and disease and ignorance and vice and paganism, saying, 'Here is where the work of Calvary Church lies.' I do not believe the real work of this church consists in having so many meetings and socials and pleasant gatherings and delightful occasions among its own members ; but the real work of this church consists in getting out of its own little circle in which it has been so many years moving, and going in any way most effective to the need of the world's wounded, to bind up the hurt and be a savior to the lost. If we do not understand this to be the true meaning of our church work then I believe we miss its whole meaning. Church work in Milton to-day does not consist in doing simply what your fathers did before you. It means helping to make a cleaner town, the purification of our municipal life, the actual planning and accomplishment of means to relieve physical distress, a thorough understanding of the problem of labor and capital, in brief, church work to-day in this town is whatever is most needed to be done to prove to this town that we are what we profess ourselves to be, disciples of Jesus Christ. That is the reason I give more time to the tenement district problem than to calling on families that are well, and in possession of great comforts and privileges. That is the reason I call on this church to do Christ's work in his name and give itself to save that unhappy part of this town."

This is but the briefest of the sketches of Phillip's sermon. It was a part of himself, his experience, his heart belief. He poured it out on the vast audience with little saving of his vitality. And that Sunday he went home at night exhausted, with a feeling of weariness partly due to his work during the week among the people. The calls upon his time and strength had been incessant, and he did not know when or where to stop.

It was three weeks after this sermon on church work that Phillip was again surprised by his strange visitor of a month before. He had been out making some visits in company with his wife.. When they came back to the house, there sat the Brother Man on the door-step.

At the sight of him Phillip felt that same thrill of expectancy which had passed over him at his former appearance.

The old man stood up and took off his hat. He looked very tired and sorrowful. But there breathed from his entire bearing the element of a perfect peace.

"Brother Man," said Phillip, cheerily, "come in and rest yourself."

"Can you keep me over night?"

The question was put wistfully. Phillip was struck by the difference between this almost shrinking request and the self-invitation of a month before.

"Yes, indeed! We have one spare room for you. You are welcome! Come in."

So they went in, and after tea Phillip and the Brother Man sat down together while Mrs. Strong was busy in the kitchen. A part of this conversation was afterwards related by the minister to his wife; a part of it he afterwards said was unreportable, — the manner of tone, the inflection, the gesture of his remarkable guest no man could reproduce.

"You have moved since I saw you last," said the visitor.

"Yes," replied Phillip. "You did not expect me to act on your advice so soon?"

"My advice?" The question came in a hesitating tone. "Did I advise you to move? Ah, yes, I remember!" A light like supremest reason flashed over the man's face and then died out. "Yes, yes, you are beginning to live on your simpler basis. You are doing as you preach. That must feel good."

"Yes," smiled Phillip, "it does feel good. Do you think, Brother Man, that this will help to solve the problem?"

"What problem?"

"Why, the problem of the church and the people, winning them, — saving them."

"Are your church-members moving out of their elegant houses and coming down here to live?" The old man asked the question in utmost simplicity.

"No; I did not ask them to do so."

"You ought to."

"What! Brother Man, do you believe my people ought literally to leave their possessions and live among the people?"

Phillip could not help asking the question, and all the time he was conscious of an absurdity mingled with a strange, unaccountable respect for his visitor, and his opinion.

"Yes," came the reply with the calmness of light. "Christ would demand it if he were pastor of Calvary Church in this age. The church-members, the Christians in this century must renounce all that they have, or they cannot be his disciples."

Phillip sat profoundly silent. The words spoken so quietly by this creature tossed upon his own soul like a vessel in a tempest. He dared not say anything for a moment. The Brother Man looked over and said at last: "What have you been preaching about since you came here?"

"A great many things."

"What are some of the things you have preached about on the first Sundays?"

"Well," Phillip clasped his hands over his knees;

" I have preached about the right and wrong uses
of property, the evil of the saloon, the Sunday as a
day of rest and worship, the necessity of moving
our church-building down into this neighborhood,
the need of living on a simpler basis, and lastly, the
true work of a church in these days."

" Has your church done what you have wished ? "

" No," replied Phillip, with a sigh.

" Will it do what you preach ought to be done?"

" I do not know."

" Why don't you resign?"

The question came with perfect simplicity, but it
smote Phillip almost like a blow. It was spoken
with calmness that hardly rose above a whisper, but
it seemed to Phillip almost like a shout. The
thought of giving up his work simply because his
church had not yet done all he wished, or because
some of his people did not like him, was the last
thing a man of his nature would do. He looked
again at the Brother Man and said : —

" Would you resign if you were in my place? "

" No." It was so quietly spoken that Phillip
almost doubted if his visitor had replied. Then he
said : " What has been done with the parsonage?"

" It is empty. The church is waiting to rent it
to some one who expects to move to Milton soon."

" Are you sorry you came here?"

" No, I am happy in my work."

" Do you have enough to eat and wear?"

" Yes, indeed, Brother Man. The thousand dollars which the church refused to take off my salary

goes to help where most needed; the rest is more than enough for us."

"Does your wife think so?" The question from any one else had been impertinent. From the Brother Man it was not.

"Let us call her in and ask her," replied Phillip, with a smile.

"Sarah, the Brother Man wants to know if you have enough to live on."

Sarah came in and sat down by Phillip. It was dusk. The year was turning into the softer months of spring, and all the out-door world had been a benediction that evening if the sorrow and poverty and sin of the tenement district so near had not pervaded the very walls and atmosphere of the entire place. The minister's wife answered bravely, "Yes, we have food and clothing and life's necessaries. But oh, Phillip, this life is wearing you out. Yes, Brother Man," she continued, while a tear rolled over her cheek, "the minister is giving his life blood to these people, and they do not care. It is a vain sacrifice." She had spoken as frankly as if the old man had been her father. There was a something in him which called out such confidence.

Phillip soothed his wife, clasping her to him tenderly. "There, Sarah, you are nervous and tired. I am a little discouraged, but strong and hearty for the work. Brother Man, you must not think we regret your advice. We have been blessed by following it."

And then their remarkable guest stretched out

his arms through the gathering gloom in the room
and seemed to bless them. Later in the evening
he again called for a Bible, and offered a prayer of
wondrous sweetness. Phillip showed him to his
plainly furnished room. The old man looked around
and smiled.

"This is like my old home," he said, — "a
palace, while the poor die of hunger."

Phillip started at the odd remark, then recol-
lected that the old man had once been wealthy,
and sometimes in his half-dazed condition Phillip
thought probable he confounded the humblest surroundings with his once luxurious home. He lingered a moment and the Brother Man said, "If
they do not renounce all they have they cannot be
my disciples."

"Good-night, Brother Man," cried Phillip as he
went out.

"Good-night, Christ's man," replied his guest.
And Phillip went to his rest that night, great questions throbbing in him and the demands of the
Master more distinctly brought to his attention than
ever.

Again, as before when he rose in the morning,
Phillip found that his visitor was gone. His eccentric movements accounted for his sudden disap-
pearances, but Phillip was disappointed. He
wanted to see his guest again and question him
about his history. He promised himself he would
do so next time.

The following Sunday Phillip preached one of

those sermons which come to a man once or twice in a whole ministry. It was the last Sunday of the month and not a special occasion. But there had surged into his thought the meaning of the Christian life with such uncontrollable power that his sermon reached hearts never before touched. He remained at the close of the service to talk with several young men, who seemed moved as never before. After they had gone away Phillip went into his own room back of the platform to get something he had left there, and to his surprise found the church sexton kneeling down by one of the chairs. As the minister came in the man rose and turned to him.

"Mr. Strong, I want to be a Christian. I want to join the church and lead a different life."

Phillip clasped the man's hand while tears rolled over his face. He stayed and talked with him and prayed with him, and when he finally went home the minister was convinced it was as strong and true a conversion as he had even seen. He at once related the story to his wife, who had gone on home to get dinner.

"Why, Phillip," she exclaimed when he said the sexton wanted to be baptized and unite with the church at the next communion, "Calvary Church never will allow him to unite with us!"

"Why not?" asked Phillip, in amazement.

"Because he is a negro!" replied his wife.

Phillip stood a moment in silence with his hat in his hand, looking at his wife as she spoke.

CHAPTER VIII

"WELL," said Phillip, slowly, as he seemed to grasp the meaning of his wife's words, "to tell the truth, I never thought of that!" He sat down and looked troubled. "Do you think, Sarah, that because he is a negro the church will refuse to receive him to membership? It would not be Christian to refuse him."

"There are other things that are Christian which the Church of Christ on earth does not do, Phillip," replied his wife, almost bitterly. "But whatever else Calvary Church may do or not do, I am very certain it will never consent to admit to membership a black man."

"But there are so few negroes in Milton that they have no church. I cannot counsel him to unite with his own people. Calvary Church *must* admit him!" Phillip spoke with the quiet determination which always marked his convictions when they were settled.

"But suppose the committee refuses to report his name favorably to the church, — what then?" Mrs. Strong spoke with a gleam of hope in her heart that Phillip would be roused to such indignation that he would resign and leave Milton.

Phillip did not reply at once. He was having an inward struggle with his sensitiveness and his interpretation of his Christ. At last he said : —

"I don't know, Sarah. I shall do what I think He would. What I shall do afterwards, that will also depend on what Christ would do. I cannot decide it yet. I have great faith in the Church on earth."

"And yet what has it done for you so far, Phillip? The business men still own and rent the saloons and gambling-houses. The money spent by the church is all out of proportion to its wealth. Here you give half your salary to build up the kingdom of God, and more than a dozen men in Calvary who are worth fifty and a hundred thousand dollars give less than a hundredth part of their incomes to Christian work in connection with the Church. It makes my blood boil, Phillip, to see how you are throwing your life away in these miserable tenements, and wasting your appeals on a church that plainly does not want to do as Christ would have it. And I don't believe it ever will."

"I'm not so sure of that, Sarah," replied Phillip, cheerfully. "I believe I shall win them yet. The only thing that sometimes troubles me is the thought, Am I doing just as Christ would do? Am I saying what he would say in this age of the world? There is one thing of which I am certain, — I am trying to do just as I believe he would. The mistakes I make are those which spring from my failure to interpret his action right. And yet I do feel deep in me that if he were pastor of this church here to-day, he would do most of the things I have done; he would preach most of the truths I have proclaimed. Don't you think so, Sarah?"

"I don't know, Phillip. Yes, I think in most things you have made an honest attempt to interpret him."

"And in the matter of the sexton, Sarah, — would n't Christ tell Calvary Church that it should admit him to its membership? Would he make any distinction of persons? If the man is a Christian, thoroughly converted, and wants to be baptized and unite with Christ's body on earth, would Christ as pastor refuse him admission?"

"There is a great deal of race prejudice among the people. If you press the matter, Phillip, I feel sure it will meet with great opposition."

"That is not the question with me. Would Christ tell Calvary Church that the man ought to be admitted? That is the question. I believe he would," added Phillip, with his sudden grasp of practical action. And Mrs. Stron knew that settled it with her husband.

It was the custom in Calvary Church for the church committee on new names for membership to meet at the minister's house on the Monday evening preceding the preparatory service. At that service all names presented to the committee were formally acted upon by the church. The committee's action was generally considered final, and the voting by the church was in accordance with the committee's report.

So when the committee came in that evening following the Sunday that had witnessed the conversion of the sexton, Phillip had ready a list of names, including those of several young men. It was a very precious list to him. It seemed almost for the first time since he came to Milton that the growing opposition to him was about to be checked, and finally submerged beneath a power of the Holy Spirit, which it was Phillip's daily prayer might come and do the work which he alone could not do. That was one reason he had borne the feeling against himself so calmly.

Phillip read the list over to the committee, saying something briefly about nearly all the applicants for membership and expressing his joy that the young men especially were coming into the church family. When he reached the sexton's name he related, simply, the scene with him after the morning service.

There was an awkward pause then. The committee was plainly astonished. Finally one said, " Brother Strong, I 'm afraid the church will object to receiving the sexton. What is his name? "

" Henry Roland."

" Why, he has been sexton of Calvary Church for ten years," said another, an older member of the committee, Deacon Stearns by name. " He has been an honest capable man. I never heard any complaint of him. He has always minded his own business. However, I don't know how the church will take it to consider him as an applicant for membership."

"Why, brethren, how can it take it in any except the Christian way?" said Phillip, eagerly. "Here is a man who gives evidence of being born again. He cannot be present to-night when the other applicants come in later, owing to work he must do, but I can say for him that he gave all evidence of a most sincere and thorough conversion; he wishes to be baptized; he wants to unite with the church. He is of more than average intelligence. He is not a person to thrust himself into places where people do not want him, — a temperate, industrious, modest, quiet workman, a Christian believer asking us to receive him at the communion table of our Lord. There is no church of his own people here. On what possible pretext can the church refuse to admit him?"

"You do not know some of the members of Calvary Church, Mr. Strong, if you ask such a question. There is a very strong prejudice against the negro in many families. This prejudice is specially strong just at this time, owing to several acts of depredation committed by the negroes living down near the railroad tracks. I don't believe it would be wise to present this name just now." Deacon Stearns appeared to speak for the committee, all of whom murmured assent in one form or another.

"And yet," said Phillip, roused to a sudden heat of indignation, "and yet what is Calvary Church doing to help to make those men down by the railroad tracks any better? Are we concerned about them at all except when our coal or wood or clothing is stolen, or some one is held up down there? And when one of them knocks at the door of the church, can we calmly shut it in his face simply because the good God made it a different color from ours?" Phillip stopped and then finished by saying very quietly, "Brethren, do you think Christ would receive this man into his Church?"

There was no reply for a moment. Then Deacon Stearns answered, "Brother Strong, we have to deal with humanity as it is. You cannot make people all over. This prejudice exists and sometimes we may have to respect it in order to avoid greater trouble. I know families in the church who will certainly withdraw if the sexton is voted in as a member. And still," said the old deacon, with a sigh, "I believe Christ would receive him into his Church."

Before much more could be said, the different applicants came, and as the custom was, after a brief talk with them about their purpose in uniting and their discipleship, they withdrew and the committee formally acted on the names for presentation to the church. The name of Henry Roland the sexton was finally reported unfavorably, three of the committee voting against it, Deacon Stearns at last voting with the minister to present the sexton's name with the others.

"Now, brethren," said Phillip, with a sad smile, as they rose to go, "you know I have always been very frank in all our relations together. And I am going to present the sexton's name to the church Thursday night and let the church vote on it in spite of the action here to-night. You know we have only recommending power. The church is the final authority. And it may accept or reject any names we present. I cannot rest satisfied until I know the verdict of the church in the matter."

"Brother Strong," said one of the committee, who had been opposed to the sexton, "you are right as to the extent of our authority. But there is no question in my mind as to the outcome of the matter. It is a question of expediency. I do not have any feeling against the sexton. But I think it would be very unwise to receive him into membership, and I do not believe the church will receive him. If you present the name, you do so on your own responsibility."

"With mine," said Deacon Stearns. He was the last to shake hands with the minister, and his warm, strong clasp gave Phillip a sense of fellowship that thrilled him with a feeling of courage and companionship very much needed. He at once went up to his study after the committee was gone. Mrs. Strong, coming up to see him later, found him as she often did now, on his knees in prayer. Ah, thou follower of Jesus in this century, what but thy prayers shall strengthen thy soul in the strange days to come?

Thursday evening was stormy. A heavy rain had set in before dark and a high wind blew great sheets of water through the streets and rattled loose boards and shingles about the tenements. Phillip would not let his wife go out; it was too stormy. So he went his way alone, somewhat sorrowful at heart as he contemplated the prospect of a small attendance on what he had planned should be an important occasion.

However, some of the best members of the church were out. The very ones that were in sympathy with Phillip and his methods were in the majority of those present, and that led to an unexpected result when the names of the applicants for membership came before the church for action.

Phillip read the list approved by the committee and then very simply but powerfully told the sexton's story and the refusal of the committee to recommend him for membership.

"Now, I do not see how we can shut this disciple of Jesus out of his Church," concluded Phillip. "And I wish to present him to this church for its action. He is a Christian; he needs our help and our fellowship; and as Christian believers, as. disciples of the Man of all the race, as those who believe that there is to be no distinction of souls hereafter that shall separate them by prejudice, I hope you will vote to receive this brother in Christ to our membership."

The voting on new members was done by ballot. When the ballots were all in and counted it was announced that all whose names were presented were unanimously elected except the sexton. There were twelve votes against him, but twenty-six for him, and Phillip declared that according to the constitution of the church he was duly elected. The meeting then went on in the usual manner characteristic of preparatory service. The sexton had been present in the back part of the room, and at the close of the meeting, after all the rest had gone, he and Phillip had a long talk with each other. When Phillip reached home he and Sarah had another long talk on the same subject. What that was we cannot tell until we come to record the events of the Communion Sunday, a day that stood out in Phillip's memory like one of the bleeding palms of the Master, pierced with sorrow but eloquent with sacrifice.

The day was beautiful, and the church as usual crowded to the doors. There was a feeling of hardly concealed excitement on the part of Calvary Church. The action of Thursday night had been sharply criticised. Very many thought Phillip had gone beyond his right in bringing such an important subject before so small a meeting of the members; and the prospect of the approaching baptism and communion of the sexton had drawn in a crowd of people who ordinarily stayed away from that service.

Phillip generally had no preaching on Communion Sunday. This morning he remained on the platform after the opening exercises and in a stillness which was almost painful in its intensity, he began to speak in a low but clear and impressive voice.

"Fellow-disciples of the Church of Christ on earth, we meet to celebrate the memory of that greatest of all beings, who on the eve of his own

greatest agony prayed that his disciples might all be
one.   In that prayer he said nothing about color or
race or difference of speech or social surroundings.
His prayer was that his disciples might all be one, —
one in their aims, in their purposes, their sympathy,
their faith, their hope, their love.

"An event has happened in this church very
recently which makes it necessary for me to say
these words.   The Holy Spirit came into this room
last Sunday and touched the hearts of several young
men who gave themselves then and here to the Lord
Jesus Christ.   Among the men was one of another
race from the Anglo Saxon.   He was a black man.
His heart was melted by the same love, his mind
illuminated by the same truth, he desired to make
confession of his belief, be baptized according to the
commands of Jesus, and unite with this church as a
humble disciple of the lowly Nazarene.   His name
was presented with the rest at the regular committee
meeting last Monday, and that committee, by a vote
of three to two, refused to present his name with
recommendations for membership.   On my own responsibility at the preparatory service Thursday night
I asked the church to act upon this disciple's name.
There was a regular quorum of the church present.
By a vote of 26 to 12 the applicant for membership
was received according to the rules of this church.

"But after that meeting the man came to me and
said that he was unwilling to unite with the church
knowing that some objected to his membership.   It
was a natural feeling for him to have.   We had a

long talk over the matter. Since then I have learned that if a larger representation of members had been present at preparatory meeting, there is a possibility that the number voting against receiving the applicant would have been much larger than those who voted for him.

"Under all these circumstances I have deemed it my duty to say what I have thus far said, and to ask the church to take the action I now propose. We are met here this morning in full membership. Here is a soul just led out of the darkness by the Spirit of truth. He is one known to many of you as an honest, worthy man, for many years faithful in the discharge of his duties in this house. There is no Christian reason why he should be denied fellowship around this table. I wish therefore to ask the members of the church to vote again on the acceptance or rejection of Henry Roland, disciple of Jesus, who has asked for admission to this body of Christ in his name. Will all those in favor of thus receiving our brother into the great family of faith signify it by raising the right hand?"

For a moment not a person in the church stirred. Every one seemed smitten into astonished inaction by the sudden proposal of the minister. Then hands began to go up. Phillip counted them, his heart beating with anguish as he foresaw the coming result. He waited a moment, it seemed to many like several minutes, and then said, "All those opposed to the admission of the applicant signify it by the same sign."

Again there was the same significant, reluctant pause. Then hands went up in numbers that almost doubled those who had voted in favor of admission. From the gallery on the sides, where several of Phillip's working-men friends sat, a hiss arose. It was slight, but heard by the entire congregation. Phillip glanced up there and it instantly ceased.

Without another word he stepped down from the platform and began to read the list of those who had been received into church-membership. He had reached the end of it when the person whose name was called last rose from his seat near the front, where all the newly received members usually sat together, and turning partly around so as to face the congregation and still address Phillip, he said :

"Mr. Strong, I do not feel, after what has taken place here this morning that I could unite with this church. This man who has been excluded from church-membership is the son of a woman born into slavery on the estate of one of my relatives. That slave woman once nursed her master through a terrible illness and saved his life. This man, her son, was then a little child. But in the strange changes that have gone on since the war, the son of the old master has been reduced to poverty and obliged to work for a living. He is now in this town. He is this very day lying upon a dying bed in the tenement district. And this black man has for several weeks out of his small earnings helped the son of his mother's old master and cared for him through his illness with all the devotion of a friend.

I have only lately learned these facts. But knowing them as I do and believing that he is as worthy to sit about this table as any Christian here, I cannot reconcile the rejection with my own purpose to unite here. I therefore desire to withdraw my application for membership. Mr. Strong, I desire to be baptized and partake of the communion as a a disciple of Christ, simply, not as a member of Calvary Church. Can I do so? "

Phillip replied in a choking voice, " You can." The man sat down. It was not the place for any demonstration, but again from the gallery came a slight but distinct note of applause. As before, it instantly subsided when Phillip looked up. For a moment every one held his breath and waited for the minister's action. Phillip's face was pale and stern. What his sensitive nature suffered in that moment no one ever knew, not even his wife, who almost started from her seat fearing that he was about to faint. For a moment there was a hesitation about Phillip's manner so unusual with him that some thought he was going to leave the church. But he quickly called on his will to assert its power, and taking up the regular communion service he calmly took charge of it as if nothing out of the way had occurred. He did not even allude to the morning's incident in his prayers. Whatever else the people might think of Phillip, they certainly could find no fault with his self-possession. His conduct of the service on that memorable Sunday was admirable.

When it was over he was surrounded by many who had taken part either for or against the sexton. There was much said about the matter. But all the arguments and excuses and comments on the affair could not remove the heart-ache from Phillip. He could not reconcile the action of the church with the spirit of the church's Master, Jesus; and when he reached home and calmly reviewed the events of the morning he was more and more grieved for the church. It seemed to him that a great mistake had been made, and that Calvary Church had disgraced the name of Christianity.

As he had been in the habit of doing since he moved into the neighborhood of the tenements, Phillip went out in the afternoon to visit the sick and troubled. The shutting down of the mills had resulted in an immense amount of suffering and trouble. As spring came on some few of the mills had opened, and men had found work in them at a reduction of wages. The entire history of the enforced idleness of thousands of men in Milton during that eventful winter would make a large volume of thrilling narrative. Phillip's story but touches on this other. He had grown rapidly familiar with the different phases of life which loafed and idled and drank itself away during that period of inaction. Hundreds of men had drifted away to other places in search of work. Almost as many more had taken to the road to swell the ever-increasing number of professional tramps, and in time to develop into petty thieves and criminals.

But those who remained had a desperate struggle with poverty. Phillip grew sick at heart as he went among the people and saw the complete helplessness, the utter estrangement of sympathy and community of feeling between the church people and the representatives of the physical labor of the world. Every time he went out to do his visiting this feeling deepened in him. This Sunday afternoon in particular it seemed to him that the depression and discouragement of the tenement district weighed on him like a great burden, bearing him down to the earth with sorrow and heart-ache.

It had been his custom to go out on Communion Sunday with the emblems of Christ to observe the rite by the bedsides of the aged or ill, or with those who could not get out to church. He carried with him this time a basket containing a part of the communion service. After going to the homes of one or two invalid church-members, he thought of the person who had been mentioned by the man in the morning as living in the tenement district and in a critical condition. He had secured his address and after a little inquiry he soon found himself in a part of the tenements new to him.

He climbed up three flights of stairs and knocked at the door. It was opened by the sexton. He greeted Phillip with glad surprise.

The minister smiled sadly.

"So, my brother, it is true you are serving your Master here? My heart is grieved at the action of the church this morning."

"Don't say anything, Mr. Strong. You did all you could. But you are just in time to see him." The sexton pointed into a small back room. "He is going fast. I did n't suppose he was so near. I would have asked you to come, but did not think he was failing so."

Phillip followed the sexton into the room. The son of the old slave-master was sinking rapidly. He was conscious, however, and at Phillip's quiet question concerning his peace with God, a smile passed over his face and he moved his lips. Phillip understood him. A sudden thought occurred to Phillip. He opened his basket, took out the bread and wine, set them on the small table and said : —

"Disciple of Jesus, would you like to partake of the blessed communion once more before you see the King in his glory?"

The gleam of satisfaction in the man's eyes told Phillip enough. The sexton said in a low voice, "He belonged to the Southern Episcopal Church in Virginia." Something in the wistful look of the sexton gave Phillip an inspiration for what followed.

"Brother," he said, turning to the sexton, "what is to hinder your baptism and partaking of the communion? Yes, this is Christ's Church wherever his true disciples are."

Then the sexton brought a basin of water; and as he kneeled down by the side of the bed, Phillip baptized him with the words, "I baptize thee, Henry, my brother, disciple of Jesus, into the name of the Father and of the Son and of the Holy Ghost ! Amen."

"Amen," murmured the man on the bed.

Then Phillip, still standing as he was, bowed his head, saying, "Blessed Lord Jesus, accept these children of thine, bless this new disciple, and unite our hearts in love for thee and thy kingdom as we remember thee now in this service."

He took the bread and said: "'Take, eat. This is my body, broken for you.' In the name of the Master who said these words, eat, remembering his love for us."

The dying man could not lift his hand to take the bread from the plate. Phillip gently placed a crumb between his lips, and then taking up the cup, he said: "In the name of the Lord Jesus, this cup is the new testament in his blood shed for all mankind for the remission of sins." He carried the cup to the lips of the man and then gave to the sexton. The smile on the dying man's face died out. The gray shadow of the last enemy was projected into the room from the setting sun of death's approaching twilight. The son of the old slave-master was going to meet the mother of the man who was born into the darkness of slavery, but born again into the light of God. Perhaps, perhaps, he thought, who knows but the first news he would bring to her would be the news of that communion? Certain it is that his hand moved vaguely over the blanket. It slipped over the edge of the bed and fell upon the bowed head of the sexton and remained there as if in benediction. And so the shadow deepened, and at last it was like unto nothing else known to the sons of men on earth, and the spirit leaped out of its clay tenement with the breath of the communion wine still on the lips of the frail, perishable body.

Phillip reverently raised the arm and laid it on the bed. The sexton rose, and while the tears rolled over his face he gazed long into the countenance of the son of his old master. No division of race now. No false and selfish prejudice here. Come! Let the neighbors of the dead come in to do the last sad offices to the casket. For the soul of this disciple is in mansions of glory, and it shall hunger no more, neither shall the darkness of death ever again smite it; for it shall live forever in the light of that Lamb of God who gave himself for the remission of sins and the life everlasting.

Phillip did what he could on such an occasion. It was not an altogether unusual event; he had prayed by many a poor creature in the clutch of the last enemy, and he was familiar with the enemy's face in the tenements. But this particular scene had a meaning and left an impression different from any he had known before. When finally he was at liberty to go home for a little rest before the evening service he found himself more than usually tired and sorrowful. Mrs. Strong noticed it as he came in. She made him lie down and urged him to give up his evening service.

"No, no, Sarah! I can't do that! I am prepared; I must preach! I'll get a nap and then I'll feel better," he said.

Mrs. Strong shook her head, but Phillip was determined. He slept a little, ate a little lunch, and when the time of service came he went up to the church again. As his habit was, just before the hour of beginning he went into the little room at the side of the platform to pray by himself. When he came out and began the service no one could have told from his manner that he was suffering physically. Even Mrs. Strong, who watched him anxiously, felt relieved to see how quiet and composed he was.

He had commenced his sermon and had been preaching with great eloquence for ten minutes, when he felt a strange dizziness and a pain in his side that made him catch his breath and clutch the side of the pulpit to keep from falling. It passed away and he went on. It was only a slight hesitation and no one remarked anything out of the way. For five minutes he spoke with increasing power and feeling. The church was filled. It was very quiet. Suddenly without any warning he threw up his arms, uttered a cry of half-suppressed agony, and then fell over backward. A thrill of excitement ran through the audience. For a moment no one moved; then every one rose. The men in the front pews rushed up to the platform. Mrs. Strong was already there. Phillip's head was raised. His old friend the surgeon was in the crowd and he at once examined him. He was not dead, and the doctor at once directed the proper steps for his removal from the church. As he was being carried out into the air he revived and was able to speak.

"'Take me home," he whispered to his wife, who hung over him in a terror as great as her love for him at that moment. A carriage was called and he was taken home. The doctor remained until Phillip was fully conscious.

"It was very warm and I was very tired and I fainted, eh, doctor? First time I ever did such a thing in my life. I am ashamed; I spoiled the service." Philip uttered this slowly and feebly when at last he had recovered enough to know where he was.

The doctor looked at him suspiciously. "You never fainted before, eh? Well, if I were you I would take care not to faint again. Take good care of him, Mrs. Strong. He needs rest. Milton could spare a dozen bad men like me better than one like the Dominie."

"Doctor!" cried Mrs. Strong, in sudden fear, "what is the matter? Is this serious?"

"Not at all. But men like your husband are in need of watching. Take good care of him."

"Good care of him! Doctor, he will not mind me! I wanted him to stay at home to-night, but he would n't."

"Then put a chain and padlock on him and hold him in!" growled the surgeon. He prescribed a medicine and went away assuring Mrs. Strong that Phillip would feel much better in the morning.

The surgeon's prediction came true. Phillip found

himself weak the next day, but able to get about. In reply to numerous calls of inquiry for the minister Mrs. Strong was able to report that he was much better. About eleven o'clock when the postman called, Phillip was in his study lying on his lounge.

His wife brought up two letters. One of them was from his old chum; he read that first. He then laid it down and opened the other.

At that moment Mrs. Strong was called downstairs by a ring at the door. When she had answered it she came upstairs again.

As she came into the room she was surprised at the queer look on Phillip's face. Without a word he handed her the letter he had just opened, and with the same look watched her face as she read it.

CHAPTER IX.

THE letter which Phillip had received and which his wife now read was as follows : —

REV. PHILLIP STRONG,
Pastor Calvary Church, Milton :

DEAR SIR AND BROTHER, — The Seminary at Fairview has long been contemplating the addition to its professorships of a chair of Sociology and Human Nature. The lack of funds and the absolute necessity of sufficient endowment for such a chair have made it impossible hitherto for the trustees to make any definite move in this direction. A recent legacy, of which you have doubtless heard, has made the founding of this new professorship possible. And now the trustees by unanimous vote have elected you as the man best fitted to fill this chair of Sociology. We have heard of your work in Milton and know of it personally. We are assured you are the man for this place. We therefore tender you most heartily the position of Professor of Sociology at Fairview Seminary at a salary of twenty five hundred dollars a year and a preliminary year's absence either abroad or in this country before you begin actual labors with the Seminary.

With this formal call on the part of the trustees goes the most earnest desire on the part of all the professors of the Seminary who remember you in your marked undergraduate success as a student here. You will meet with the most loving welcome, and the Seminary will be greatly strengthened by your presence in this new department.

We are, in behalf of the Seminary,

Very cordially yours, THE TRUSTEES.

Here followed their names, familiar to both Phillip and his wife.

There was a moment of astonished silence and then Sarah said : —

" Well, Phillip, that 's what I call the finger of Providence ! "

" Do you call it the finger of Providence because it points the way you want to go?" asked Phillip, with a smile. But his face instantly grew sober. He was evidently very much excited by the call to Fairview. It had come at a time when he was in a condition to be very much moved by it.

" Yes, Phillip," replied his wife, as she smoothed back his hair from his forehead, " it is very plain to me that you have done all that any one can do here in Milton, and this call comes just in time. You are worn out. The church is opposed to your methods. You need a rest and a change. And besides, this is the very work that you have always had a liking for."

Phillip said nothing for a moment. His mind was in a whirl of emotion. Finally he said, "Yes, I should enjoy such a professorship. It is a very tempting call. I feel drawn towards it. And yet," — he hesitated, — " I don't know that I ought to leave Milton just now."

Mrs. Strong was provoked. "Phillip Strong, you have lived this kind of life long enough! All your efforts in Calvary Church are wasted. What good have all your sermons done? It is all a vain sacrifice, and the end will be defeat and misery for you. Add to all this the fact that this new work will call for the best and most Christian labor, and that some good Christian man will take it if you don't, — and I don't see, Phillip, how you can possibly think of such a thing as refusing this opportunity."

"It certainly is a splendid opportunity," murmured Phillip. "I wonder why they happened to pitch on me for the place!"

"That's easy enough. Every one knows that you could fill that chair better than almost any other man in the country."

"Do you mean by 'every one' a little woman named Sarah?" asked Phillip, with a brief return of his teasing habit.

"No, sir, I mean all the professors and people in Fairview and all the thinking people of Milton and every one who knows you, Phillip. Every one knows that whatever else you lack it isn't brains."

"I'd like to borrow some just now, though, for I seem to have lost most of mine. Lend me yours, won't you, Sarah, until I settle this question of the call?"

"No, sir, if you can't settle a plain question like this with all your own brains you couldn't do any better with the addition of the little I have."

"Then you really think, do you, Sarah, that I

ought to accept this as the leading of the Spirit of God, and follow without hesitation."

Mrs. Strong replied with almost tearful earnestness :

"Phillip, it seems to me like the leading of his hand. Surely you have shown your willingness and your courage and your self-sacrifice by your work here. But your methods are distasteful, and your preaching has so far roused only antagonism. Oh, I dread the thought of this life for you another day. It looks to me like a suicidal policy, with nothing to show for it when you have gone through it."

Phillip spread the letter out on the couch and his face grew more and more thoughtful as he gazed into the face of his wife, and his mind went over the ground of his church experience. If, only, he was perhaps thinking, if only the good God had not given him so sensitive and fine-tempered a spirit of conscientiousness. He almost envied men of coarse, blunt feelings, of common ideals of duty and service.

His wife watched him anxiously. She knew it was a crisis with him. At last he said : —

"Well, Sarah, I don't know but you're right. The spirit is willing, but the flesh is weak. The professorship would be free from the incessant worry and anxiety of a parish, and then I might be just as useful in the Seminary as I am here, — who knows?"

"Who knows, indeed ! " exclaimed Sarah, joyfully ; at the same time she was almost crying. She picked up the letter and called Phillip's attention to the clause which granted him a year abroad in case he accepted. "Think of it, Phillip! Your dream of foreign travel can come true now."

"That is," Phillip looked out of the window over the dingy roof of a shed near by the gloomy tenements, "that is, supposing I decide to accept."

"Supposing! But you said, in effect — Oh, Phillip, say you will! Be reasonable! This is the opportunity of a lifetime!"

"That 's true," replied Phillip.

"You may not have another such chance as this as long as you live. You are young now and with every prospect of success in work of this kind. It is new work, of the kind you like. You will have leisure and means to carry on important experiments, and influence for life young men entering the ministry. Surely, Phillip, there is as great opportunity for usefulness and sacrifice here as anywhere. It must be that the will of God is in this. It comes without any seeking on your part."

"Yes, indeed!" Phillip spoke with the only touch of pride he ever exhibited. It was pride in the knowledge that he was absolutely free from self-glory or self-seeking.

"Then say you will accept. Say you will, Phillip!"

The appeal, coming from the person dearest to him in all the world, moved Phillip profoundly. He took the letter from her hand, read it over carefully, and again laid it down on the couch. Then he said: —

"Sarah, I must pray over it. I need a little time. You will have reason — " Phillip paused, as his manner sometimes was, and at that moment the bell rang and Mrs. Strong went downstairs. As she went along she felt almost persuaded that Phillip would yield. Something in his tone seemed to imply that the struggle of his mind was nearly ended.

The callers at the door were three men who had been to see Phillip several times to talk with him about the mill troubles and the labor conflict in general. They wanted to see Phillip. Mrs. Strong was anxious about the condition of Phillip's health. She asked the men to come in, and went upstairs again.

"Can you see them? Are you strong enough?" she asked.

"Yes, tell them to come up. I am comfortable now."

Phillip was resting easily, and after a careful look at him Mrs. Strong went downstairs.

To her surprise two of the men had gone. The one who remained explained that he thought three persons would excite or tire the minister more than one; that he had stayed and would not trouble Phillip long. But the business on which he came was of such an important nature that he felt obliged to see the minister if he could do so without danger to him.

So the man went up and Phillip greeted him with his usual heartiness, excusing himself for not rising.

The man took a chair, moved up near the couch, and sat down. He seemed a good deal excited, but in a suppressed and cautious way.

"I came to see you, Mr. Strong, to tell you about a thing you ought to know. There is danger of your life here."

"Where?" asked Phillip, calmly.

"Here, in this neighborhood."

"Well?" Phillip waited for more explanation.

"I did n't want to tell your wife, for fear of scaring her, but I thought you ought to know, Mr. Strong, and then you could take steps to protect yourself or get away."

"Go on; tell me the worst," said Phillip, quietly, as the man paused.

"Well," the man went on in a low tone, "two others and me overheard a talk last night by the men who run the Star Saloon and den down by the Falls. They have a plan to waylay and rob and injure you, sir, — and do it in such a way as to make it seem like a common hold-up. They seemed to know about your habit of going around through the alleys and cross-streets of the tenements. We heard enough to make us sure they really and truly meant to deal foul by you first good chance, and thought best to put you on your guard. The rummies are down on you, Mr. Strong, you have been so outspoken against them; and your lecture in the hall last week has made them mad, I tell you. They hate you worse than poison, for that's the article they seem to sell and make a living out of."

Phillip had the week before addressed a large gathering of working-men, and in the course of his speech he had called attention to the saloon as one of the greatest pests of the wage-earner.

" Is that all? " Phillip asked.

" All, man alive ! — is n't it enough? What more do you hanker after? "

" Of course I don't ' hanker after ' being held up or attacked, but these men are mistaken if they think to frighten me."

" They mean more than frighten, Mr. Strong. They mean business."

" Why don't you have them arrested, then, for con-spiracy? If you overheard them talk they are guilty and could be convicted."

" Not in Milton, Mr. Strong. Besides, there was no name mentioned. And the talk was scattering-like. They are shrewd devils. But we could tell they meant you plain enough, — not to prove anything in court though."

" And you came to warn me? That was kind of you, my brother ! " Phillip spoke with the winsome affection for men that enabled him to " grapple them to his soul with hoops of steel."

" Yes, Mr. Strong, and I tell you the rummies will almost hold a prayer-meeting when you leave Milton. And they mean to make you trouble enough until you do leave. If I was you," the man paused curiously, — " if I was you I 'd get up and leave this God-forsaken town, Mr. Strong."

" You would? " Phillip glanced at the letter

which still lay open on the couch beside him. "Suppose I should say I had about made up my mind to do just that thing?"

"Oh, no, Mr. Strong, you don't mean that!" The man made a gesture toward Phillip that revealed a world of longing and hunger for fellowship that made Phillip's heart throb with a feeling of intense joy mingled with an ache of pain. The man at once repressed his emotion. It had been like a lightning-flash out of a summer cloud.

"Yes," said Phillip, as if continuing, "I have been thinking of leaving Milton."

"That might be best. You're in danger here. No telling when some harm may come to you."

"Well, I'm thinking I might as well leave. My work here has been a failure, anyway."

"What! A failure? Mr. Strong, you don't know the facts. There has never been a minister in Milton who did so much for the poor and the working-man as yourself! Let me tell you," the man continued with an earnestness that concealed an emotion he was trying to subdue, "Mr. Strong, if you were to leave Milton now it would be a greater loss to the common people than you can imagine. You may not know it, but your influence among us is very great. I have lived in Milton as boy and man for thirty years, and I never knew so many laboring-men attend church and the lectures in the hall as during the few months you have been here. Your work here has not been a failure; it has been a great success."

A tear stole out of Phillip's eye and rolled down and fell with a warm splash on the letter which lay beside him. If a twenty-five-hundred-dollar call could be drowned by one tear that professorship in Sociology in Fairview Seminary was in danger.

" So you think the people in this neighborhood would miss me a little? " He asked almost as modestly as if he were asking a great favor.

" Would they, Mr. Strong ! You will never know what you have done for them. If the mill-men were to hear of your leaving they would come down here in a body and almost compel you to stay. I cannot bear to think of your going. And yet the danger you are in, the whiskey men — "

Phillip roused himself up, interrupting his visitor. The old-time flash of righteous indignation shot out of his eye as he exclaimed : " I am more than half-minded to stay just on that account ! The rummies would think they had beaten me out if I left ! "

" Oh, Mr. Strong, I can't tell you how glad we would be if you would only stay ! And yet — "

" And yet," replied Phillip, with a sad smile, " there are many things to take into the account. I thank you out of my heart for the love you have shown me. It means more than words can express." And Phillip leaned back with a wearied look on his face, which, nevertheless, revealed his deep satisfaction at the thought of such friendship as this man had for him.

He was getting exhausted with the interview, following so soon on his illness of the night before. The visitor was quick to notice it, and after a warm clasp of hands he went away. Phillip, lying there alone while his wife was busy downstairs, lived an age in a few minutes. All his life so far in Milton, the events of his preaching and his experiences in the church, his contact with the workmen, his evident influence over them, the thought of what they would feel in case he left Milton to accept this new work, the dissatisfaction at the thought of an uncompleted work abandoned, the thought of the exultation of the whiskey men, — all this and much more surged in and out of his mind and heart like heavy tides of a heaving ocean as it rushes into some deep fissure and then flows back again with noise and power. He struggled up into a sitting position, and with pain of body almost fell from the couch upon his knees, and with his face bowed upon the letter, which he spread out before him with both hands, he sobbed out a yearning cry to his Master for light in his darkness.

It came as he kneeled there; and it did not seem to him at all strange or absurd that as he kneeled, there came to his thought a picture of the Brother Man. And he could almost hear the Brother Man say: "Your work is in Milton, in Calvary Church yet. Except a man shall renounce all that he hath he cannot be His disciple." It mattered not to Phillip that the answer to his prayer came in this particular way. He was not superstitious or morbid, or given to yielding to impulse or fancy. He lay down upon the couch again and knew in his heart that he was at peace with God and his own conscience in deciding to stay with Calvary Church and refuse the call to Fairview.

When, a few minutes later, Mrs. Strong came up Phillip told her exactly how he had decided.

"I cannot leave these poor fellows in the tenements yet; my work is just beginning to count with them. And the church, oh, Sarah, I love it, for it has such possibilities and it *must* yield in time; and then the whiskey men, — I cannot bear to have them think me beaten, driven out, defeated. And in addition to all the rest I have a feeling that God has a wonderful blessing in store for me and the church very soon; and I cannot banish the feeling that if I should accept the call to Fairview I should always be haunted by that ghost of Duty murdered and run away from which would make me unhappy in all my future work. Dear little woman," Phillip went on, as he drew his wife's head down and kissed her tenderly, while tears of disappointment fell from her, — "little woman, you know you are the dearest of all earthly beings to me. And my soul tells me the reason you loved me enough to share earth's troubles with me was that you knew I could not be a coward in the face of my duty, my conscience, and my God. Is it not so?"

The answer came in a sob of mingled anguish and happiness: —

"Yes, Phillip, but it was only for your sake I

wanted you to leave this work. It is killing you. Yet" (and she lifted her head with a smile through all the tears), — "yet, Phillip" (she quoted from Ruth's words to Naomi), " ' whither thou goest I will go, and where thou lodgest I will lodge ; thy people shall be my people, and thy God my God. Where thou diest will I die, and there will I be buried ; the Lord do so to me and more also if aught but death part thee and me.' "

There were people in Milton who could not understand how a person of such refined and even naturally expensive and luxurious habits as the minister's wife possessed could endure the life he had planned for himself, and his idea of Christian living in general. Phillip could have told them if he had been so minded. And this scene could have revealed it to any one who knew the minister and his wife as they really were. That was a sacred scene to husband and wife, something that belonged to them, one of those things which the world did not know and had no business to know.

When the first Sunday of another month had come Phillip felt quite well again. A rumor of his call to Fairview had gone out, and to the few intimate friends who asked him about it he did not deny, but he said little. The time was precious to him. He plunged into the work with an enthusiasm and a purpose which sprang from his knowledge that he was at last gaining some influence in the tenement district.

The condition of affairs in that neighborhood was growing worse instead of better. The amount of

vice and drunkenness and crime and brutality made
Phillip's sensitive heart quiver a hundred times a
day as he went his way through it all. His study
of the whole question led him to the conviction
that one of the great needs of the place was a new
home life for the people. The tenements were
owned and rented by men of wealth and influence.
Many of these men were in the church. Discouraged as he had so far been in his endeavor to get
the moneyed men of the congregation to consecrate
their property to Christian uses, Phillip came up to
that first Sunday with a new phase of the same
great subject which pressed so hard for utterance
that he could not keep it back.

As he faced the church this morning he faced an
audience composed of very conflicting elements.
Representatives of labor were conspicuous in the
galleries. People whom Phillip had assisted at one
time and another were scattered about through the
house, mostly in the back seats under the choir
gallery. His own membership was represented by
men who, while opposed to his idea of the Christian
life and his interpretation of Christ, nevertheless continued to go and hear him preach. The incident of
the sexton's application for membership and his rejection by vote had also told somewhat in favor of
Phillip. Very many preachers would have resigned
after such a scene. Phillip had said his say about
it, and then refused to speak or be interviewed by
the papers on the subject. But this morning as he
rose to give his message in the person of Christ, the

thought of the continued suffering and shame and degradation in the tenement district, the thought of the great wealth in the possession of the church which might be used to transform the lives of thousands of people, if the men of riches in Calvary Church would only see the kingdom of God in its demands on them, — this voiced Phillip's cry to the people, and gave his sermon the significance and solemnity of a prophet's inspiration.

"See !" he exclaimed, as he went on after drawing a vivid picture of the miserable condition of life in the buildings which could not be called homes, "see what a change could be made by the use of a few thousand dollars down there. And here this morning in this house men are sitting who own very many of those tenements, who are getting the rent from them every month, who could, without depriving themselves of one necessity or even luxury of life, so change the surroundings of these people that they would enjoy the physical life God has given them, and be able to see his love in the lives of his disciples. O my brethren, is not this your opportunity? What is money compared with humanity? What is the meaning of our discipleship unless we are using what God has given us to build up his kingdom? The money represented by this church could rebuild the entire tenement district. The men who own these buildings," Phillip paused as if he had suddenly become aware that he might be saying an unwise thing ; then after a brief hesitation, as if he had satisfied his own doubt, he repeated,

"The men who own these tenements (and members of other churches are among the owners) are guilty in the sight of God for allowing human beings in his image to grow up in such horrible surroundings when it is in the power of money to stop it. Therefore they shall receive greater condemnation at the last, when Christ sits on the throne of the universe to judge the world. For will he not say, as he said long years ago, 'I was hungry and ye gave me no meat, naked and ye clothed me not, sick and in miserable dwellings reeking with filth and disease, and ye drew the hire of these places and visited me not'? For are these men and women and children not our brethren? Verily, God will require it at our hands, O men of Milton, if, having the power to use God's property so as to make the world happier and better, we refused to do so and went our ways careless of our own responsibility, and selfish in our use of God's money."

Phillip closed his sermon with an account of facts concerning the condition of some of the people he himself had visited. When the service closed, more than one property owner went away secretly enraged at Phillip's bold, and as most of them said and thought, 'impertinent meddling in their business.' Was Phillip wise? And yet he had gone to more than one of these men in private with the same message. Had he not the right to speak in public? Did not Christ do so? Would he not do so if he were here on earth again? And Phillip, seeing the great need, seeing the mighty power of money, seeing the indifference of these men to the whole matter, seeing their determination to conduct their business for the gain of it without regard to the condition of life, — Phillip, with his heart sore and his soul indignant at the suffering he had witnessed, came into the church and flung his sword of wrath out of its scabbard, smiting at the very thing dearest of all things to thousands of church-members to-day, — the money, the property, the lust of acquisition ; and he smote perhaps with a somewhat unwise energy of denunciation, yet with his heart crying out for wisdom with every blow he struck, "Would Christ say it? Would he say it?" And his sensitive, keenly sensitive spirit heard the answer, "Yes, I believe he would." Back of that answer Phillip did not go in those days so rapidly drawing to their tremendous close. He bowed the soul of him to his Master and said, "Thy will be done!"

The week following this Sunday was one of the busiest Phillip had known. With the approach of warmer weather, a great deal of sickness came on. He was going early and late on errands of mercy to the poor souls all about his own house. The people knew him now and loved him. He comforted his spirit with that knowledge as he prayed and worked.

He was going through one of the narrow courts one night on his way home, with his head bent down and his thoughts on some scene of suffering, when he was suddenly confronted by a man who stepped quickly out from a shadowed corner, threw one arm about Phillip's neck and placed his other hand over his mouth and attempted to throw him over backward.

It was very late, and no one was in sight. Phillip said to himself, " This is the attack of which I was warned." He was taken altogether by surprise, but being active and self-possessed, he sharply threw himself forward, repelling his assailant's attack, and succeeded in pulling the man's hand away from his mouth. His first instinct was to cry out for help ; his next was to keep still. He suddenly felt the other giving way. The assailant's strength seemed to be leaving him. Phillip, calling up some of his knowledge of wrestling gained while in college, threw his entire weight upon him, and to his surprise the man offered no resistance. They both fell heavily upon the ground, the stranger underneath. He had not spoken and no one had yet appeared. As the man lay there motionless, Phillip rose and stood over him. By the dim light that partly illuminated the court from a street lamp farther on, Phillip saw that his assailant was stunned. There was a pump not far away. Phillip went over and brought some water. After a few moments the man recovered consciousness. He sat up and looked about in a confused manner. Phillip stood near by, looking at him thoughtfully.

CHAPTER X

A S the man looked up at Phillip in a dazed condition, Phillip said slowly: —

"You're not hurt badly, I hope. Why did you attack me?"

The man seemed too bewildered to answer. Phillip leaned over and put one arm about him to help him to rise. He struggled to his feet, but almost instantly sat down on the curb at the side of the road, holding his head between his hands. For a moment Phillip hesitated. Then he sat down beside the man, and after finding out that he was not seriously hurt succeeded in drawing him into a conversation which grew more and more remarkable as it went on. As he recalled it afterward, Phillip was unable to account exactly for the way in which the confidence between him and his assailant had been brought about. The incident and all that followed from it has such a bearing on the crucifixion that it belongs to the whole story.

"Then you say," went on Phillip after they had been talking in brief question and answer for a few minutes, "you say that you meant to rob me, taking me for another man?"

"Yes, I thought you was the mill-man, — what is his name? — Winter."

" Why did you want to rob him?" Phillip asked, not knowing just what to say.

The man replied, harshly, almost savagely, "Because he has money and I was hungry."

" How long have you been hungry?"

" I have not had anything to eat for almost three days."

" There is food to be had at the Poor Commissioners. Did you know that fact?"

The man did not answer, and Phillip asked him again. The reply came in a tone of bitter emphasis that made the minister start : —

" Yes, I knew it ! I would starve before I would go to the Poor Commissioners for food."

" Or steal?" asked Phillip, gently.

" Yes, or steal. Would n't you?"

Phillip stared out into the darkness of the court and answered honestly : "I don't know."

There was a short pause. Then Phillip asked :

" Can't you get work?"

It was a hopeless question to put to a man in a town of over two thousand idle men. The answer was what Phillip knew it would be : —

" Work ! Can I pick up a bushel of gold in the street out there? Can a man get work where there ain't any?"

" What have you been doing?"

" I was fireman in the Lake Mills. Good job. Lost it when they closed down last winter."

" What have you been doing since?"

" Anything I could get."

"Are you a married man?"

The question affected the other strangely. He trembled all over, put his head between his knees, and out of his heart's anguish flowed the words, " I had a wife. She's dead, — of consumption. I had a little girl. She's dead too. Thank God!" exclaimed the man, with a change from a sob to a curse. "Thank God! — and curses on all rich men who had it in their power to prevent the hell other people feel on earth, and which they will feel for themselves in the other world!"

Phillip did not say anything for some time. What could any man say to another at once under such circumstances? Finally he said : —

" What will you do with money if I give you some?"

" I don't want *your* money," replied the man.

" I thought you did a little while ago," said Phillip, simply.

" It was the mill-owner's money I wanted. You're the preacher, aren't you, up at Calvary Church?"

"Yes. How did you know?"

" I've seen you. Heard you preach once. I never thought I should come to this, — holding up a preacher down here!" And the man laughed a hard, short laugh.

"Then you're not — " Phillip hardly knew how to say it. He wanted to say that the man was not connected in any way with the saloon element; "you're driven to this desperate course on your own account? The reason I ask is that I have been threatened by the whiskey men and at first I supposed you were one of them."

"No, sir," was the answer, almost in disgust. "I may be pretty bad, sir, yet not so low as that."

"Then your only motive was hunger?"

"That was all. Enough, ain't it?"

"We can't discuss the matter here," said Phillip. He hesitated, rose, and stood there looking at the man who sat now with his head resting in his arms, which were folded across his knees. Two or three persons came out of a street near by and walked past. Phillip knew them and said good-evening. They thought he was helping some drunken man, a thing Phillip had often done, and they went along without stopping. Again the street was deserted.

"What will you do now?" asked Phillip. "Where will you go?"

"God knows. I am an outcast on his earth!"

"Have you no home?"

"Home! Yes; the gutter, the street, the bottom of the river."

"My brother!" Phillip laid his hand on the man's shoulder, "come home with me, have something to eat, and stay with me awhile."

The man looked up and stared at Phillip through the semi-darkness.

"What, go home with you! That would be a good one after trying to hold you up! I 'll tell you what you ought to do. Take me to the police station and have me arrested for attempt at highway robbery. Then I'd get lodgings and victuals for nothing."

Phillip smiled slightly. "That would not help matters any. And if you know me at all you know I would never do any such thing. Come home with me. No one except you and myself need ever know what has happened to-night. I have food at my home, and you are hungry. We both belong to the same Father-God. Why should I not help you if I want to?"

It was all said so calmly, so lovingly, so honestly that the man softened under it. A tear rolled over his cheek. He brushed his hand over his eyes. It was a long time since any one had called him "brother."

"Come!" Phillip reached out his hand and helped him to rise. The man staggered, and might have fallen if Phillip had not supported him. "I am faint and dizzy," he said.

"Courage now! My home is not far off; we shall soon be there," said Phillip, cheerfully. His companion was silent. As they came up to the door Phillip said, "I have n't asked your name, but it might save a little awkwardness if I knew it."

"William — " Phillip did not hear the last name, it was spoken in such a low voice.

"Never mind; we'll call you William if it's all the same to you." And Phillip went into the house with the man, and at once made him feel at home by means of that simple and yet powerful spirit of brotherhood which was ready to level all false distinctions, and which possibly saw in prophetic vision the coming event in his own career when all distinctions of title and name would be as worthless as dust in the scales of eternity.

Mrs. Strong at once set food upon the table, and then she and Phillip with true delicacy busied themselves in another room so as not to watch the man while he ate. When he had satisfied his hunger Phillip showed him the little room where the Brother Man had stayed one night.

"You may make it your own as long as you will," Phillip said. "You may look upon it as simply a part of what has been given us to be used for the Father's children."

The man seemed dazed by the result of his encounter with the preacher. He murmured something about thanks. He was evidently very much worn, and the excitement of the evening had given place to an appearance of dejection that alarmed Phillip. After a few words he went out and left the man, who said that he felt very drowsy.

"I believe he is going to have a fever or something," Phillip said to his wife as he joined her in the other room. He related his meeting with the man, making very light of his attack and indeed excusing it on the ground of his desperate condition.

"What shall we do with him, Phillip?"

"We must keep him here until he finds work. I believe this is one of the cases that call for personal care. We cannot send him away; the man's entire future depends on our treatment of him. But I don't like his looks; I fear he is going to be a sick man."

Phillip's fear was realized. The next morning he found his lodger in the clutch of a fever. Before night he was delirious. And Phillip, with the burden of his work weighing heavier on him every moment, took up this additional load and prayed his Lord to give him strength to carry it and save another soul.

It was at the time of this event in Phillip's life that another occurred which had its special bearing upon the crisis of all his life.

The church was dear to his thought, loved by him with a love that only very few of the members understood. In spite of his apparent failure to rouse the church to a conception of her duty as he saw it, Phillip was confident that the spirit of God would accomplish the miracle which he could not do. Then there were those in Calvary Church who sympathized heartily with him and were ready to follow his leadership. He was not without fellowship, and it gave him courage. Add to that the knowledge that he had gained a place in the affection of the working-people, and that was another reason why Phillip kept up good heart and did not let his personal sensitiveness enter too largely into his work. It was of course impossible for him to hide from himself the fact that very many members of the church had been offended by much that he had said and done. But he was the last man in the

world to go about his parish trying to find out the
quantity of opposition that existed. His Sunday
congregation crowded the church. He was popular
with the masses. Whenever he lectured among
the working-men the hall was filled to overflowing.
He could not acknowledge even to himself that the
church could long withstand the needs of the age
and the place. He had an intense faith in it as an
institution. He firmly believed all it needed was to
have the white light of truth poured continually on
the Christ as he would act to-day, and the church
would respond, and at last in a mighty tide of love
and self-sacrifice throw itself into the work the church
was made to do.

So he began to plan for a series of Sunday-night
services different from anything Milton had ever
known. Phillip's life in the tenement district
and his growing knowledge of the labor world had
convinced him of the fact that the church was
missing its opportunity in not grappling with the
problem as it existed in Milton. It seemed to him
that the first step to a successful solution of that
problem as far as the church was concerned was for
the church and the working-man to get together
on some common platform for a better mutual
understanding. He accordingly planned for a series
of Sunday-night services, in which his one great purpose was to unite the church and the labor unions
in a scheme of mutual helpfulness. His plan was
very simple. He invited into the meeting one or
two thoughtful leaders of the mill-men and asked

them to state in the plainest terms the exact condition of affairs in the labor world from their standpoint. Then Phillip, for the church, took up their statements, their complaints, or the reasons for their differences with capital, and answered them from the Christian standpoint: What would Christ advise under these circumstances? He had different subjects presented on different evenings. One night it was reasons why the mill-men were not in the church. Another night it was the demand of men for better houses, and how to get them. Another night it was the subject of strikes and the attitude of Christ on wages and the relative value of the wage-earners' product and the capitalists' intelligence. At each meeting Phillip allowed one or two of the invited leaders to take the platform and say very plainly what to his mind was the cause and what the remedy for the poverty and crime and suffering of the world. Then he closed the evening's discussion by a calm, clear statement of what was to him the direct application of Jesus' teaching to the point at issue.

Finally, as this series drew to a close at the end of the month, a subject came up which roused intense feeling. It was the subject of wealth, its power, responsibility, meaning, and Christian use. The church was jammed in every part of it. The services had been so unusual, the conduct of them had so often been intensely practical, the points made had so often told against the existing Church that great mobs of mill-men filed into the room and

for the time being took possession of Calvary
Church. For the four Sunday nights of that series
Phillip faced great crowds, mostly of grown-up men,
crowds that his soul yearned over with unspeakable
emotion, wonderful audiences for Calvary to witness, the like of which Milton had never seen.

We cannot do better than give the evening
paper's account of this last service in the series.
With one or two slight exaggerations the account
was a faithful picture of one of the most remarkable
meetings ever held in Milton. The paper, after
speaking of the series as a sensational departure
from the old church methods, went on to say :

" It will be safe to say that those who were fortu-
nate enough to secure standing-room in Rev. Mr.
Strong's church last night heard and saw things that
no other church in this town ever witnessed.

" In the first place, it was a most astonishing
crowd of people. Several of the church-members
were present, but they were in the minority. The
mill-men swarmed in and took possession. It is
not exactly correct to say that they lounged on the
easy-cushioned pews of the Calvary Church, for there
was not room enough to lounge, but they filled up
the sanctuary and seemed to enjoy the comfort and
luxury of it.

" The subject of the evening was Wealth, and the
President of the Trades Assembly of Milton made a
statement of the view which working-men in general
have of wealth as related to labor of hand or brain.
He stated what to his mind was the reason for the

discontent of so many at the sight of great numbers of rich men in times of suffering, or sickness, or lack of work. 'Why, just look at the condition of things here and in every large place all over the world,' he said. Men are suffering for the lack of common necessaries while men of means with money in the bank continue to live just as luxuriously and spend just as much as they ever did for things not needful for happiness. It was in the power of the men of wealth in Milton to prevent most if not all of the suffering here this last winter and spring. It was in their power to see that the tenements were better built and arranged for health and decency. It was in their power to do a thousand things that money and money alone can do, and I believe they will be held to account for not doing some of those things!'

"At this point some one in the gallery shouted out, 'Hang the aristocrats!' Instantly Rev. Mr. Strong rose and stepped to the front of the platform. Raising his long, sinewy arm and stretching out his open hand in appeal, he said, while the great audience was perfectly quiet, 'I will not allow any such disturbance at this meeting. We are here, not to denounce people, but to find the truth. Let every fair-minded man bear that in mind.'

"The preacher sat down, and the audience cheered. Then before the President of the Assembly could go on, a man rose in the body of the house and asked if he might say a word.

"Mr. Strong said he might if he would be brief.

The man then proceeded to give a list of people
who, he said, were becoming criminals because they
could n't get work. After he had spoken a minute
Rev. Mr. Strong asked him to come to the point and
show what bearing his facts had on the subject of
the evening. The man seemed to become confused,
and finally his friends or the people near him pulled
him down, and the President of the Trades Assembly resumed the discussion, closing with the statement that never in the history of the country had
there been so much money in the banks and so
little of it in the pockets of the people ; and when that
was a fact something was wrong ; and it was for the
men who owned the money to right that wrong, for
it lay in their power, not with the poor man.

" He was followed by a very clear and intensely
interesting talk by Rev. Mr. Strong on the Christian
teaching concerning the wealth of the world. Several times he was interrupted by applause, once with
hisses, several times with questions. He was hissed
when he spoke of the great selfishness of the labor
unions and trades organizations in their attempts to
dictate to other men in the matter of work. With
this one exception, in which the reverend gentleman
spoke with his usual frankness, the audience cheered
his presentation of the subject, and was evidently
in perfect sympathy with his views. Short extracts
from his talk will show the drift of his entire belief
on this subject : —

" ' Every dollar that a man earns should be spent
to the glory of God.

" 'The teaching of Christianity about wealth is the same as about anything else ; it all belongs to God, and should be used by the man as God would use it in the man's place.

" 'It is a great mistake which many people make, church-members among the rest, that the money they get is their own to do with as they please. Men have no right to use anything as they please unless God pleases so too.

" 'The accumulation of vast sums of money by individuals or classes of men has always been a bad thing for society. A few very rich men and a great number of very poor men is what gave the world the French Revolution and the guillotine.

" 'There are certain conditions true of society at certain times when it is the Christian duty of the rich to use every cent they possess to relieve the need of society. Such a condition faces us to-day.

" 'The foolish and unnecessary expenditure of society on its trivial pleasures at a time when men and women are out of work and children are crying for food is a cruel and unchristian waste of opportunity.

" 'If Christ were here to-day I believe he would tell the rich men of Milton that every cent they have belongs to Almighty God, and they are only trustees of his property.

" 'This is the only true use of wealth : that the man who has it recognize its power and privilege to make others happy, not provide himself luxury.

" 'The church that thinks more of fine architecture and paid choirs than of opening its doors to the people that they may hear the gospel, is a church that is mortgaged for all it is worth to the devil, who will foreclose at the first opportunity.

" ' The first duty of every man who has money is to ask himself, What would Christ have me do with it? The second duty is to go and do it, after hearing the answer.

" ' If the money owned by church-members were all spent to the glory of God there would be fewer hundred-thousand-dollar churches built and more model tenements.

" ' If Christ had been a millionnaire he would have used his money to build up character in other people, rather than build a magnificent brown-stone palace for himself. But we cannot imagine Christ as a millionnaire.

" ' It is just as true now as when Paul said it nearly twenty centuries ago : " The love of money is a root of all kinds of evil ; " it is the curse of our civilization, the greatest passion of the human race to-day.

" ' Our civilization is only partly Christian. For Christian civilization means more comforts ; ours means more wants.

" ' If a man's pocket-book is not converted with his soul the man will not get into heaven on it.

" ' There are certain things that money alone can secure ; but among those things it cannot buy is character.

" ' All wealth, from the Christian standpoint, is in

the nature of trust funds, to be so used by the admin-istrator as God, the owner, shall direct. No man owns the money for himself. The gold is God's, the silver is God's! That is the plain and repeated teaching of the Bible.

"'It is not wrong for a man to make money. It is wrong for him to use it selfishly or foolishly.

"'If consecrated, the wealth of the men of Milton could provide work for every idle man in town. The Christian use of the wealth of the world would make impossible the cry for bread.

"'Most of the evils of our present condition flow out of the love of money. The almighty dollar is the God of Protestant America.

"'If men loved men as eagerly as they love money the millennium would be just around the corner.

"'Wealth is a curse unless the owner of it blesses the world with it.

"'"If any man hath the world's goods, and seeth his brother have need, and shutteth up his compas-sion from him, how dwelleth the love of God in him?"

"'Christian Socialism teaches a man to bear other people's burdens. The very first principle of Christian Socialism is unselfishness.

"'We shall never see a better condition of affairs in this country until the men of wealth realize their responsibility and privilege.

"'Christ never said anything against the poor as a class. He did speak some tremendous warnings in the face of the selfish rich.

" ' The only safe thing for a man of wealth to do
is to ask himself, What would Christ do with my
money if he had it?

" ' Everything a man has is God's. On that pre-
found principle the whole of human life should rest.
We are not our own; we have been bought with a
price.'

" It would be impossible to describe the effect of
the Rev. Mr. Strong's talk upon the audience. Once
the applause was so long continued that it was a full
minute before he could go on. When he closed
with a tremendous appeal to the wealth of Milton to
use its power for the good of the place, for the tear-
ing down and remodelling of the tenements, for the
solution of the problem of work for thousands of
desperate men, the audience rose to their feet and
cheered again and again.

" At the close of the meeting the minister was surrounded by a crowd of men, and an after meeting
was held, at which steps were taken to form a committee composed of prominent church people and
labor leaders to work if possible together toward a
common end.

" It was rumored yesterday that several of the leading members of Calvary Church are very much dissatisfied with the way things have been going during
these Sunday-evening meetings, and are likely to
withdraw if they continue. They say that Mr.
Strong's utterances are socialistic and tend to in-
flame the minds of the people to acts of violence.
Since the attack on Mr. Winter nearly every mill-

owner in town goes armed and takes extra precau-
tions. Mr. Strong was much pleased with the result
of the Sunday-night meetings and said they had done
much to bridge the gulf between the church and the
people. He refused to credit the talk about dis-
affection in Calvary Church."

In another column of this same paper were five
separate accounts of the desperate condition of
affairs in the town. The midnight hold-up attacks
were growing in frequency and in boldness. In
addition to all the other troubles, the sickness in the
tenement district had assumed the nature of an
epidemic of fever, clearly caused by the lack of
sanitary regulations, imperfect drainage, and crowding of families. Clearly the condition of matters
was growing serious.

At this time the ministers of different churches in
Milton held a meeting to determine on a course of
action that would relieve some of the distress.
Various plans were submitted. Some proposed dis-
tricting the town to ascertain the number of needy
families. Others proposed a union of benevolent
offerings to be given the poor. Another group suggested something else. To Phillip's mind not one
of the plans submitted went to the root of the matter.
He was not in favor with the other ministers. Most
of them thought he was sensational. A good many
were jealous of his popularity. However, Phillip
made a plea for his own plan, which was radical and
as he believed went to the real heart of the subject.
He proposed that every church in town, regardless

of its denomination, give itself in its pastor and members to the practical solution of the social troubles by personal contact with the suffering and sickness in the district; that the churches all throw open their doors every day in the week, week-days as well as Sundays, for the discussion and agitation of the whole matter; that the county and the State be petitioned to take speedy action toward providing necessary labor for the unemployed; and that the churches cut down all unnecessary expenses of paid choirs, abolish pew rents, urge wealthy members to consecrate their riches to the solving of the problem, and in every way, by personal sacrifice and common union, work and pray and sacrifice as a unit, to make themselves felt as a real power on the side of the people in their present great need. It was Christian America, but Phillip's plan was not adopted. It was discussed with some warmth, but declared to be visionary, impracticable, unnecessary, not for the church to undertake, beyond its function, etc. Phillip was disappointed, but he kept his temper.

" Well, brethren," he said, "what can we do to help the solution of these questions? Is the church of America to have no share in the greatest problem of human life that agitates the world to-day? Is it not true that the people in this town regard the Church as an insignificant organization unable to help at this crisis in the affairs of the people, and the preachers as a lot of weak, impractical men, with no knowledge of the real state of affairs? Are we not divided over our denominational differences when we ought to be united in one common work for the saving of the whole man? I have not any faith in the plan proposed to give our benevolence or to district the town and visit the poor. All those things are well enough in their place. But matters are in such shape here now and all over the country that we must do something larger than that. We must do as Christ would if he were here. What would he do? Would he give anything less than his whole life to it? Would he not give himself? The Church as an institution is facing the greatest opportunity it ever saw. If we do not seize it on the largest possible scale we shall miserably fail of doing our duty."

When the meeting adjourned Phillip was aware he had simply put himself out of touch with the majority present. They did not, they could not look upon the Church as he did. A committee was appointed to investigate the matter and propose a plan of action at the next meeting in two weeks. And Phillip went home smiling almost bitterly at the little bulwark which Milton churches proposed to rear against the tide of poverty and crime and drunkenness and political chicanery and wealthy selfishness. To his mind it was a house of paper cards in the path of a tornado.

Saturday night Phillip was out calling a little while, but he came home early. It was the first Sunday of the month on the morrow, and he had not fully prepared his sermon. As he came in, his wife met him with a look of news on her face.

"Guess who is here?" she said in a whisper.

"'The Brother Man," replied Phillip, quickly.

"Yes, but you never can guess what has happened. He is in there with William. And the Brother Man, — Phillip, it seems like a chapter out of a novel, — the Brother Man has discovered that William is his only son, who cursed his father and disowned him when he gave away his property. They are in there together. I could not keep the Brother Man out."

Phillip and Sarah stepped to the door of the little room, which was open, and looked in.

The Brother Man was kneeling at the side of the bed praying, and his son was listening, with one hand tight-clasped in his father's, while the large tears were rolling over his pale face.

CHAPTER XI

WHEN the Brother Man had finished his prayer he rose, and stooping over his son he kissed him. Then he turned about and faced Phillip and Sarah, who almost felt guilty of intrusion in looking at such a scene. But the Brother Man wore a radiant look. To Phillip's surprise he was not excited. The same ineffable peace breathed from his entire person. To that peace was now added a fathomless joy.

"Yes," he said very simply, "I have found my son which was lost. God is good to me. He is good to all his children. He is the All-Father. He is Love."

"Did you know your son was here?" Phillip asked.

"No, I found him here. You have saved his life. That was doing as He would."

"It was very little we could do," said Phillip, with a sigh. He had seen so much trouble and suffering that day that his soul was sick within him. Yet he welcomed this event in his house. It seemed a little like the brightness of heaven on earth.

The sick man was too feeble to talk much. The tears and the hand-clasp with his father told the story of his reconciliation, of the bursting out of the old love, which had not been extinguished, only smothered for a time. Phillip thought best for the patient that he should not become excited with the meeting, and in a little while drew the Brother Man out into the other room.

By this time it was nearly ten o'clock. The old man stood hesitating in a curious fashion when Phillip asked him to be seated. And as before, he asked if he could find a place to stay over night.

"You have n't room to take me in," he said when Phillip urged his welcome upon him.

"Oh, yes, we have. We 'll fix a place for you somewhere. Sit right down, Brother Man."

The old man at once accepted Phillip's invitation and sat down. Not a trace of anxiety or hesitation remained. The peacefulness of his demeanor was restful to the weary Phillip.

"How long has your son," Phillip was going to say, "been away from home?" Then he thought it might offend the old man, or that possibly he might not wish to talk about it. But he quietly replied : —

"I have not seen him for five years. He was my youngest son. We quarrelled. All that is past. He did not know that to give up all that one has is the will of God. Now he knows. When he is well we will go away together." The Brother Man spread out his palms in his favorite gesture, with plentiful content in his face and voice.

Phillip was on the point of getting his strange guest to tell something of his history, but his great weariness and the knowledge of the strength needed for his Sunday work checked the questions that rose for answer. Mrs. Strong also came in and insisted that Phillip should get the rest he so much needed. She arranged a sleeping-place on a lounge for the Brother Man, who, after once more looking in upon his son and assuring himself that he was resting, lay down with a look of great content upon his beautiful face.

In the morning Phillip almost expected to find that his visitor had mysteriously disappeared, as on the other occasions. And he would not have been so very much surprised if the Brother Man had vanished, taking with him his son. But it was that son who now kept the Brother Man at Phillip's house; and in the simplest fashion he stayed on, nursing the sick man, who recovered very slowly. A month passed by after the Brother Man had first found the lost at Phillip's house, and he was still a guest there. Within that month great events crowded in upon the experience of Phillip. To tell them all would be to write another story. Sometimes in men's lives, under certain conditions of society, or of men's own mental and spiritual relation to certain courses of action, time, as reckoned by days or weeks, cuts no figure. A man can live an eternity in an hour. He feels it. It was so with Phillip. We have spoken of the rapidity of his thought in deciding questions of right or expediency. The same habit of mind caused a possibility in him of condensed experience. In a few days he reached the conclusions of a year's thought. That month, while the Brother Man was peacefully watching by the side of the patient, and relieving Mrs. Strong and a neighbor who had helped before he came, Phillip fought some tremendous battles with himself, with his thought of the church, and with the world around. It is necessary to understand something of this in order to comprehend the meaning of his last Sunday in Milton, — a Sunday that marked an era in the place, from which the people almost reckoned time itself.

As spring had blossomed into summer every one had predicted better times. But the predictions did not bring them. The suffering and sickness and helplessness of the tenement district grew every day more desperate. To Phillip this district seemed like the ulcer of Milton. All the surface remedies proposed and adopted by the city council and the churches and the benevolent societies had not touched the problem. The mills were going on part time. Thousands of men yet lingered in the place hoping to get work. Even if the mills had been running as usual that would not have diminished by one particle the sin and vice and drunkenness that saturated the place. And as Phillip studied the matter with brain and soul he came to a conclusion regarding the duty of the church. He did not pretend to go beyond that, but as the weeks went by and autumn came on and another winter stared the people coldly in the face, Phillip knew that he must speak out what burned in him.

He had been a year in Milton now. Every month of that year had impressed Phillip with the width and apparent hopelessness of the chasm that yawned between the working world and the church. There was no point of contact. One was suspicious, the other was indifferent. Something was radically wrong, and something radically positive and Christian must be done to right the condition that faced the churches of Milton. That was in Phillip's soul as he went his way like one of the old prophets, imbued with the love of God as he saw it in the heart of Christ. With infinite longing he yearned to bring the church to a sense of her great power and opportunity. So matters had finally drawn to a point in the month of November. The Brother Man had come in October. The sick man recovered slowly. Phillip and his wife found room for the father and son, and shared with them what comforts they had. It should be said that after moving out of the parsonage into his home in the tenement district, Phillip had given more than the extra thousand dollars the church insisted on paying him. The demands on him were so urgent, the perfect impossibility of providing men with work and so relieving them had been such a bar to giving help in that direction, that out of sheer necessity, as it seemed to him, Phillip had given fully half of the thousand dollars which at first he reserved for his own expenses. His entire expenses were reduced to the smallest possible amount. Everything above that went where it was absolutely needed. He was

literally sharing what he had with the people who
had not anything. It seemed to him that he could
not consistently do anything less in view of what he
had preached.

One evening in the middle of the month he was
invited to a social gathering at the house of Mr.
Winter. The mill-owner had of late been expe-
riencing a revolution of thought. His attitude
toward Phillip had grown more and more friendly.
Phillip welcomed the rich man's change of feeling
toward him with an honest joy at the thought that
the time might come when he would see his privilege and power, and use both to the glory of Christ's
kingdom. He had more than once helped Phillip
lately with sums of money for the relief of destitute
cases, and a feeling of mutual confidence was growing up between the men.

Phillip went to the gathering with the feeling that
a change of surroundings and thought would do him
good. Mrs. Strong, who for some reason was detained at home, urged Phillip to go, thinking the
social evening spent in bright and luxurious surroundings would be a rest to him from his incessant
labors in the depressing atmosphere of poverty and
disease.

It was a gathering of personal friends of Mr.
Winter, including some of the church people. The
moment that Phillip stepped into the spacious hall
and caught a glimpse of the furnishings of the rooms
beyond, the contrast between all the comfort and
brightness of this house and the last place he had

visited in the tenement district smote him with a sense of pain. He drove it back and blamed himself with an inward reproach that he was growing narrow and could think of only one idea.

Phillip could not remember just what brought up the subject, but some one during the evening, which was passed in conversation and music, mentioned the rumor going about of increased disturbance in the lower part of the town, and carelessly wanted to know if the paper did not exaggerate the facts. Some one turned to Phillip and asked him about it as the one best informed. Phillip had been talking with an intelligent lawyer who had been reading a popular book which Phillip had also reviewed for a magazine. He was thoroughly enjoying the talk, and for the time being the human problem which had so long wearied his heart and mind was forgotten.

He was roused out of this to answer the question concerning the real condition of affairs in the lower part of the town. Instantly his mind sprang back to that which absorbed it in reality more than anything else. Before he knew it he had not only answered the particular question, but had gone on to describe the picture of desperate life in the tenement district. The buzz of conversation in the other rooms gradually ceased. The group about the minister grew, as others became aware that something unusual was going on in that particular room. Phillip unconsciously grew eloquent and his handsome face lighted up with the fires that raged deep in him at the thought of diseased and de-

praved humanity. He did not know just how long
he talked. He knew there was a great hush when
he had ended. Then before any one could change
the stream of thought some young woman in the
music-room who had not known what was going
on began to sing to a new instrumental variation
" Home, Sweet Home." Coming as it did after
Phillip's vivid description of the tenements, it
seemed like a sob of despair or a mocking hypocrisy. Phillip drew back into one of the smaller
rooms and began to look over some art prints on a
table. As he stood there, again blaming himself
for his impetuous breach of society etiquette in
almost preaching on such an occasion, Mr. Winter
came in and said : —

"It does not seem possible that such a state of
affairs exists as you describe, Mr. Strong. Are you
sure you do not exaggerate ? "

" Exaggerate ! Mr. Winter, you have pardoned
my little sermon here to-night, I know. It was forced
on me. But — " Phillip choked, and then with an
energy that was all the stronger for being repressed,
he said, turning full toward the mill-owner, " Mr.
Winter, will you go with me and look at things for
yourself? In the name of Christ will you see how
humanity is sinning and suffering not more than a
mile from this home of yours ? "

Mr. Winter hesitated and then said, " Yes, I 'll
go. When ? "

" Say to-morrow night. Come down to my house
early and we will start from there."

Mr. Winter agreed, and when Phillip went home he glowed with hope. If once he could get people to know for themselves it seemed to him the fulfilment of his desire for needed co-operation would follow.

When Mr. Winter came down the next evening, Phillip asked him to come in and wait a few minutes, as he was detained in his study-room by a caller. The mill-owner sat down and chatted with Mrs. Strong a little while. Finally she was called into the other room and Mr. Winter was left alone. The door into the sick man's room was partly open, and the mill-owner could not help hearing the conversation between the Brother Man and his son. Something said made Mr. Winter curious, and when Phillip came down he asked him a question concerning his strange boarder.

"Come in and see him," said Phillip.

He brought Mr. Winter into the little room and introduced him to the patient. He was able to sit up now. At mention of Mr. Winter's name he flushed and trembled. It then occurred to Phillip for the first time that it was the mill-owner that his assailant that night had intended to waylay and rob. For a second the minister was very much embarrassed. Then he recovered himself, and after a few quiet words with Brother Man he and Mr. Winter went out of the room to start on their night visit through the tenements.

As they were going out of the house the patient called Phillip back. He went in again and the man said, "Mr. Strong, I wish you would tell Mr. Winter all about it."

" Would you feel easier? " Phillip asked gently.

" Yes."

" All right; I 'll tell him, — don't worry. Brother Man, take good care of him. I shall not be back until late." He kissed his wife and joined Mr. Winter, and together they made the round of the district.

As they were going through the court near by the place where Phillip had been attacked, he told the mill-owner the story. It affected him greatly; but as they went on through the tenements the sights that met him there wiped out the recollection of everything else.

It was all familiar to Phillip; but it always looked to him just as terrible. The heart-ache for humanity was just as deep in him at sight of suffering and injustice as if this had been the first instead of the hundredth time he had ever seen them. But to the mill-owner the whole thing came like a revelation. He had not dreamed of such a condition as possible.

" How many people are there in our church that know anything about this plague spot from personal knowledge, Mr. Winter? " Phillip asked after they had been out about two hours.

" I don't know. Very few, I presume."

" And yet they ought to know about it. How else shall all this sin and misery be done away? "

" I suppose the law could do something," replied the mill-owner, feebly.

"The law!" Phillip said the two words and then stopped. They stumbled over a heap of refuse thrown out into the doorway of a miserable structure. "Oh, what this place needs is not law and ordinances and statutes so much as live, loving Christian men and women who will give themselves and a large part of their means to cleanse the souls and bodies and homes of this wretched district. We have reached a crisis in Milton when Christians must give themselves to humanity! Mr. Winter, I am going to tell Calvary Church so next Sunday."

Mr. Winter was silent. They had come out of the district and were walking along together toward the upper part of the city. The houses kept growing larger and better. Finally they came up to the avenue where the churches were situated, — a broad, clean, well-paved street with magnificent elms and elegant houses on either side and the seven large, beautiful church-buildings with their spires pointing upward, almost all of them visible from where the two men stood. They paused there a moment. The contrast, the physical contrast was overwhelming to Phillip, and to the wealthy mill-man coming from the unusual sights of the lower town it must have stood out with a new meaning.

A door in one of the houses near by opened. A group of people passed in. The glimpse caught by the two men was a glimpse of bright, flower-decorated rooms, beautiful dresses, glittering jewels, and a table heaped with delicacies. It was the Paradise of Society, the display of its ease, its soft enjoyment of pretty things, its careless indifference to humanity's pain in the lower town. The group of new-comers went in, a strain of music and the echo of a dancing laugh floated out into the street, and then the door closed.

Mr. Winter and Phillip went on. Phillip had his own reason for accompanying the other home, and Mr. Winter was secretly glad of his presence, for he was timid at night alone in Milton. He broke a long silence by saying : —

" Mr. Strong, if you preach to the people to leave such pleasure as that we have just glanced at to view or suffer such things as we found in the tenements, you must expect opposition. I doubt if they will understand your meaning. I know they will not do any such thing. It is asking too much."

" And yet the Lord Jesus Christ ' although he was rich, for our sakes became poor, that we, through his poverty, might be rich.' Mr. Winter, what this town needs is that kind of Christianity, — the kind that will give up the physical pleasures of life to show the love of Christ to perishing men. I believe it is just as true now as when Christ lived, that unless they are willing to renounce all that they have, they cannot be his disciples."

" Do you mean literally, Mr. Strong? " asked the rich man after a little.

" Yes, *literally*, sometimes. I believe the awful condition of things and souls we have witnessed to-night will not be any better until many, many of the professing Christians in this town and in Calvary

Church are willing to leave, actually to leave their beautiful homes and spend the money they now spend in luxuries for the good of the weak and poor and sinful."

"Do you think Christ would preach that if he were in Milton?"

"I do. It has been burned into me that he would. I believe he would say to the members of Calvary Church, 'If any man love houses and money and society and power and position more than me, he cannot be my disciple.' And then he would test the entire church by its willingness to renounce all these physical things. And if he found the members willing, if he found that they loved him more than the money or the power, he might not demand a literal giving up. But he would say to them, 'Take my money and my power, for it is all mine, and use them for the building up of my kingdom.' He would not then perhaps command them to leave literally their beautiful surroundings. And then in some cases I believe that he would. Oh, yes! — sacrifice! sacrifice! What does the Church in America in this age of the world know about it? How much do church-members give themselves nowadays to the Master? That is what we need, — *self*, the souls of men and women, the living sacrifices for those lost children down yonder! Oh, God! — to think of what Christ gave up! And then to think of how little his Church is doing to obey his last command to go and make disciples of the nations!"

Phillip strode through the night almost forgetful of his companion. By this time they had reached Mr. Winter's house. Very little was said by the mill-owner. A few brief words of good-night, and Phillip started for home. He went back through the avenue on which the churches stood. When he reached Calvary Church he went up on the steps and prayed. Great sobs shook him. They were sobs without tears, — sobs that were articulate here and there with groans of anguish and desire. He prayed for his loved church, for the wretched beings in the hell of torment, without God and without hope in the world, for the spirit of Christ to come again into the heart of the church and teach it the meaning and extent of sacrifice.

When at last he rose and came down the steps it was very late. The night was cold, but he did not feel it. He went home. He was utterly exhausted. He felt that the burden of the place was wearing him out and crushing him into the earth. He wondered if he was beginning to know ever so little what a tremendous invitation that was : " Come unto me all ye that labor and are heavy laden, and I will give you rest." *All!* The weary, sinful souls in Milton were more than he could carry. He shrank back before the amazing spectacle of the mighty Burden-Bearer of the sin of all the world, and fell down at his feet and breathed out the words, " My Lord and my God ! " before he sank into a heavy sleep.

When the eventful Sunday came he faced the

usual immense concourse. He did not come out of the little room until the last moment. When at length he appeared, his face bore marks of tears. At last they had flowed as a relief to his soul, and he gave the people his message with a courage and a peace and a love born of direct communion with the Spirit of Truth.

As he went on, people began to listen in amazement. He had begun by giving them a statement of facts concerning the sinful, needy, desperate condition of life in the place. He then rapidly sketched the contrast between the surroundings of the Christian and those of the non-Christian people, between the working-men and the church-members. He stated what was the fact in regard to the unemployed and the vicious and the ignorant and the suffering. And then with his heart going out to the people, he spoke the words which aroused the most intense astonishment : —

" Disciples of Jesus," he exclaimed, " the time has come when our Master demands of us some token of our discipleship greater than the giving of a little money or a little work and time to the solution of the great problem of modern society and of our own city. The time has come when we must give ourselves. The time has come when we must renounce, if it is best, if Christ asks it, the things we have so long counted dear, the money, the luxury, the homes even, and go down into the tenement district to live there and work there with the people. I do not wish to be misunderstood here. I

do not believe our modern civilization is an absurdity. I do not believe Christ if he were here
to-day would demand of us foolish things. But this
I do believe he would require, — ourselves. We
must give ourselves in some way that will mean real,
genuine, downright, and decided self-sacrifice. If
Christ were here he would say to some of you, as he
said to the young man, "Sell all you have and give
to the poor, and come, follow me." And if you were
unwilling to do it he would say you could not be his
disciples. The test of discipleship is the same now
as then; the price is no less on account of the
lapse of two thousand years. Eternal life is something which has only one price, and that is the same
always.

"What less can we do than give ourselves and all
we have to the salvation of souls in this city? Have
we not enjoyed our pleasant things long enough?
What less would Christ demand of the church to-
day than the giving up of its unnecessary luxuries,
the consecration of every dollar to his glory and the
throwing of ourselves on the altar of his service?
Members of Calvary Church, I solemnly believe the
time has come when it is our duty to go into the
tenement district and redeem it by the power of
personal sacrifice. Nothing less will answer. To
accomplish this great task, to bring back to God
this great part of his kingdom, I believe we ought
to spend our time, our money, and ourselves. It is
a sin for us to live at our pleasant ease, in enjoyment of all good things, while men and women and

children by the thousand are dying, body and soul, before our very eyes in need of the blessings of Christian civilization in our power to share with them. We cannot say it is not our business. We cannot excuse ourselves on the plea of business. This is our first business, — to love God and man with all our might. This problem before us calls for all our Christian discipleship. Every heart in this church should cry out this day, "Lord, what wilt thou have me to do?" And each soul must follow the commands that honestly he hears. But out of the depths of the black abyss of human want and sin and despair and anguish and rebellion in this place and over the world rings in my ear a cry for help that by the grace of God I truly believe cannot be answered by the Church of Christ on earth until the members of that Church are willing in great numbers to give all their money and all their time and all their homes and all their luxuries and all their accomplishments and all their artistic tastes and all themselves to satisfy the needs of the generation as it looks for the heart of the bleeding Christ in the members of the Church of Christ. Yea, truly, except a man is willing to renounce all that he hath, he cannot be his disciple. Does Christ ask any member of Calvary Church to renounce all and go down into the tenement district to live Christ there? I believe he does. Literally? Yes.

"Ah, my beloved, if Christ speaks so to you to-day, listen and obey. Service! Self! That is what he wants. And if he asks for *all*, when all is needed, what then? Can we sing that hymn with any Christian honesty of heart unless we interpret it literally? —

> " 'Were the whole realm of nature mine,
>   That were an offering far too small;
> Love so amazing, so divine,
>   Demands my soul, my life, my *all!* ' "

It would partly describe the effect of this sermon on Calvary Church to state the fact that when Phillip ended and then kneeled down by the side of the desk to pray, the silence was painful and the intense feeling provoked by his remarkable statements was felt in the appearance of the audience as it remained seated after the benediction. But the ultimate effect was yet to show itself; it was not visible in the Sunday audience.

The next day Phillip was unexpectedly summoned out of Milton to the parish of his old college chum. His old friend was thought to be dying. He had sent for Phillip on that supposition. Phillip, whose affection for him was second only to that which he gave his wife, went at once. His friend was almost gone. He rallied when Phillip came, and then for two weeks his life swung back and forth between this world and the next. Phillip stayed on and so was gone one Sunday from his pulpit in Milton. Then the week following, as Alfred gradually came back from the shore of that other world, Phillip, assured that he would live, returned home.

During that ten days' absence serious events had taken place in Calvary Church. Phillip reached home on Wednesday. He at once went to the house and greeted his wife and the Brother Man, and William, who was now sitting up in the large room.

Phillip had not been home more than an hour when the greatest drowsiness and dizziness came over him. He had sat up much with his chum and was entirely worn out. He went upstairs to lie down on his couch in his small study. He instantly fell asleep and dreamed that he was standing on the platform of Calvary Church. He thought he said something the people did not like. Suddenly a man in the audience raised a revolver and fired it at him. At once, from all over the house, people aimed revolvers at him and began to fire. The noise was terrible, and in the midst of it he awoke to feel to his amazement that his wife was kneeling at the side of the couch, sobbing with a heart-ache that was terrible to him; he was instantly wide awake and her dear head clasped in his arms. And when he prayed her to tell him the matter, she sobbed out the news to him which her faithful, loving heart had concealed from him while he was at the bedside of his friend. And even when the news of what the church had done in his absence had come to him fully through her broken recital of it, he did not realize it until she placed in his hands the letter which the congregation had voted to be written, asking him to resign his pastorate of Calvary Church. Even then he fingered the envelope in an absent way, and for an instant his eyes left the bowed form of his wife and looked out beyond the sheds over to the tenements. Then he opened the letter and read it.

CHAPTER XII

PHILLIP read the letter through without lifting his eyes from the paper or making any comment. It was as follows: —

REV. PHILLIP STRONG,

Calvary Church, Milton:

DEAR SIR, — As clerk of the church I am instructed to inform you of the action of the church at a regularly called meeting, held last Thursday night. At that meeting it was voted by a majority present that you be asked to resign the pastorate of Calvary Church for the following reasons: —

1. There is a very wide-spread discontent on the part of the church-membership on account of the use of the church for Sunday-evening discussions of social, political, and economic questions, and the introduction into the pulpit of persons whose character and standing are known to be hostile to the church and its teachings.

2. The business men of the church, almost without exception, are agreed, and so expressed themselves at the meeting, that the sermon of Sunday before last was exceedingly dangerous in its tone, and liable to lead to the gravest results in acts of lawlessness and anarchy on the part of people who are already inflamed to deeds of violence against property and wealth. Such preaching, in the opinion of the majority of pew-owners and supporters of Calvary Church, cannot be allowed, or the church will inevitably lose its standing in society.

3. It is the fixed determination of a majority of the oldest and most influential members of Calvary Church

to withdraw from the organization all support under the present condition of affairs. The trustees announced that the pledges for church support had already fallen off very largely, and last Sunday less than half the regular amount was received. This was ascribed to the sermon of the first of the month.

4. The vacation of the parsonage and the removal of the minister into the region of the tenement district has created an intense feeling on the part of a large number of families who have for years been firm supporters and friends of the church. They feel that the action was altogether uncalled for, and they think that it has been the means of disrupting the church and throwing matters into confusion, besides placing the church in an unfavorable light with the other churches and the community at large.

5. It was the opinion of a majority of the members present that while much of the spirit exhibited by yourself was highly commendable, yet in view of all the facts it would be expedient for the pastoral relation to be severed. The continuance of that relation seemed to promise only added disturbance and increased antagonism in the church. It was the well-nigh unanimous verdict that your plans and methods might succeed to your better satisfaction with a constituency made up of non-church people, and that possibly your own inclinations would lead you to take the step which the church has thought wisest and best for all concerned.

It is my painful duty as the clerk of Calvary Church to write thus plainly the action of the church and the specific reasons for that action. A council will be called to review our proceedings and advise with reference to the same.

In behalf of the church,

CALVIN SMITH, *Clerk.*

Phillip finished the letter and lifted his eyes again. And again he looked out through the window across the sheds to the roofs of the tenements. From where he sat he could also see, across the city, up on the rising ground, the spire of Calvary Church. It rose distinct and cold against the gray December sky. The air was clear and frosty, the ground was covered with snow, and the roofs of the tenements showed black and white patches where the thinner snow had melted. He was silent so long that his wife became frightened.

"Phillip! Phillip!" she cried, as she threw her arms about his neck and drew his head down nearer. "They have broken your heart! They have killed you! There is no love in the world any more!"

"No! No!" he cried suddenly. "You must not say that! You make me doubt. There is the love of Christ, which passeth knowledge. But oh, for the Church! — which he loved and for which he gave himself!"

"But it is not the Church of Christ that has done this thing, Phillip."

"Nevertheless it is the Church in the world," he replied. "Tell me, Sarah, how this was kept so secret from me."

"You forget. You were so entirely absorbed in the care of Alfred; and then the church meeting was held with closed doors. Even the papers did not know the whole truth at once. I kept it from you as long as I could!"

"Little woman," spoke Phillip, very gently and

calmly, "this is a blow to me. I did not think the church would do it. I hoped — " he paused and his voice trembled for a brief moment, then grew quiet again, "I hoped I was gradually overcoming opposition. It seems I was mistaken. It seems I did not know the feeling in the church."

He looked out of the window again and was silent. Then he asked, "Are they *all* against me?" The question came with a faint smile that was far more heart-breaking to his wife than a flood of tears. She burst into a sob.

"No, you have friends. Mr. Winter fought for you, — and others."

"Mr. Winter! — my old enemy! That was good. And there were others?"

"Yes, quite a number. But nearly all the influential members were against you. Phillip, you have been blind to all this."

"Do you think so?" Phillip asked simply. "Maybe that is so. I have not thought of people so much as of the work which needed to be done. I have tried to do as my Master would have me. But I have lacked wisdom, or tact, or something."

"Phillip, it is not that. Do you want to know what I believe?" His wife fondly stroked the hair back from his forehead, as she sat on the couch by him.

"Yes, little woman, tell me." To Phillip's eyes his wife never seemed so beautiful or dear as now. He knew that they were one in this their hour of trouble.

" Well, I have learned to believe since you came to Milton that if Jesus Christ were to live on the earth in this century and become the pastor of almost any large and wealthy or influential church and preach as he would have to, the church would treat him just as Calvary Church has treated you. The world would crucify Jesus Christ again even after two thousand years of historical Christianity."

Phillip did not speak. He looked out again toward the tenements. The winter day was drawing to its close. The church spire still stood out sharp against the sky. Finally he turned to his wife, and with almost a groan he uttered the words : " Sarah, I do not like to believe it. The world is full of the love of Christ. It is not the same world as Calvary saw."

" No, Phillip. But by what test are nominal Christians and church-members tried to-day? Is not the church in America and England a church in which the scribes and pharisees, hypocrites, are just as certainly found as they were in the old Jewish church? And would not that element crucify Christ again if he spoke as plainly now as then ? "

Again Phillip looked out of the window. His whole nature was shaken to its foundation. Repeatedly he drove back the thought of the church's possible action in face of the Christ of this century. As often it returned and his soul cried out in anguish at the suggestion of the truth. Even with the letter of Calvary Church before him he was slow to believe that the Church as a whole or in a majority of cases would reject the Master.

"I have made mistakes. I have been lacking in tact. I have needlessly offended the people," he said to his wife, yielding almost for the first time to a great fear and distrust of himself. For the letter asking his resignation had shaken him as once he thought impossible. "I have tried to preach and act as Christ would; but I have failed to interpret him aright. Is it not so, Sarah?"

His wife was reluctant to speak. But her true heart made answer: "No, Phillip, you have interpreted him too faithfully. You may have made mistakes; all ministers do; but I honestly believe you have preached as Christ would against the great selfishness and hypocrisy of the century. The same thing would have happened to him."

They talked a little longer, and then Phillip said : —

"Let us go down and see the Brother Man. Somehow I feel inclined to talk with him."

So they went downstairs and into the room where the invalid was sitting with the old man. William was able to walk about now, and had been saying that he wanted to hear Phillip preach as soon as he could get to the church.

"Well, Brother Man," said Phillip, with something like his old heartiness of manner, "have you heard the news? Othello's occupation 's gone."

The Brother Man seemed to know all about it. Whether he had heard of it through some of the

church people or not, Mr. Strong did not know.
The old man looked at Phillip calmly. There was
loving sympathy in his voice, but no trace of compassion or wonder. Evidently he had not been
talking of the subject to any one.

"I knew it would happen," he said. "You have
offended the rulers."

"What would you do, Brother Man, in my
place? Would you resign?" Phillip remembered
the time when the Brother Man had asked him why
he did not resign.

"Don't they ask you to?"

"Yes."

"Do you think it is the wish of the whole
church?"

"No, there are some who want me to stay."

"How do you feel about it?" The Brother Man
put the question almost timidly. Phillip replied
without hesitation : —

"There is only one thing for me to do. It would
be impossible for me to remain after what has been
done."

The Brother Man nodded his head as if in
approval. He did not seem disturbed in the least.
His demeanor was the most perfect expression of
peace that Phillip ever saw.

"We shall have to leave Milton, Brother Man,"
said Phillip, thinking that possibly he did not understand the meaning of the resignation.

"Yes, we will go away together. Together."
The Brother Man looked at his son and smiled.

"Mr. Strong," said William, "we cannot be a burden on you another day. I am able to get out now, and I will find work somewhere and provide for my father and myself. It is terrible to me to think of how long we have been living on your slender means." And William gave Phillip a look of gratitude and love that made Phillip's heart warm again.

"My brother, we will see to that all right. You have been more than welcome. Just what I will do, I don't know, but I am sure the way will be made clear in time, are n't you, Brother Man?"

"Yes, the road to heaven is always clear," he said, almost singing the words.

"We shall have to leave this house, Brother Man," said Sarah, feeling with Phillip that he did not grasp the meaning of the event.

"Yes, in the Father's house are many mansions," replied the Brother Man. Then as Phillip and his wife sat there in the gathering gloom the old man said suddenly, "Let us pray together about it."

He kneeled down and offered the most remarkable prayer that Phillip had ever heard. It seemed to him that however the old man's mind might be affected, the part of him that touched God in the communion of audible prayer was absolutely free from any weakness or disease. It was a prayer that laid its healing balm on the soul of Phillip and soothed his trouble into peace. When the old man finished, Phillip felt almost cheerful again. He went out and helped his wife a few minutes in some work about the kitchen. And after supper he was just getting ready to go out to inquire after a sick family near by, when there was a knock at the door.

It was a messenger boy with a telegram. Phillip opened it almost mechanically and carrying it to the light read : —

"Alfred died four P. M. Can you come?"

For a second, Phillip did not realize the news. Then as it rushed upon him, he staggered and would have fallen if the table had not been so close. A faintness and a pain seized him and for a minute he thought he was falling. Then he pulled himself together and called his wife, who was in the kitchen. She came in at once, noticing the peculiar tone of his voice.

"Alfred is dead!" He was saying the words quietly as he held out the telegram.

"Dead! And you left him getting better! How dreadful!"

"Do you think so? He is at rest. I must go up there at once; they expect me." He still spoke quietly, stilling the tumult of his heart's anguish for his wife's sake. This man, his old college chum, was very dear to him. The news was terrible to him.

Nevertheless, he made his preparations to go back to his friend's home. It is what either would have done in the event of the other's death. And so he was gone from Milton until after the funeral, and did not return until Saturday. In those three days of absence Milton was stirred by events that grew out of the action of the church.·

In the first place the minority in the church held

a meeting and voted to ask Phillip to remain, pledging him their hearty support in all his plans and
methods. The paper, in its report of this meeting,
made the most of the personal remarks that were
made, and served up the whole affair in sensational
items, that were eagerly read by every one in Milton.

But the most important gathering of Phillip's
friends was that of the mill-men. They met in the
hall where he had so often spoken, and being
crowded out of that by the great numbers, they secured the use of the court house. This was crowded
with an excited assembly, and in the course of very
many short speeches in which the action of the church
was severely condemned, a resolution was offered
and adopted asking Phillip to remain in Milton and
organize an association or something of a similar
order for the purpose of sociological study and agitation, pledging whatever financial support could be
obtained from the working-people. This also was
caught up and magnified in the paper, and the town
was still roused to excitement by all these reports
when Phillip returned home late Saturday afternoon,
almost reeling with exhaustion, and his heart torn
with the separation from his old chum.

However, he tried to conceal his weariness from
Sarah, and partly succeeded. After supper he went
up to his study to prepare for the Sunday. He had
fully made up his mind as to what he would do, and
he wanted to do it in a manner that would cast
no reproach on his profession, which he sincerely
respected.

He shut the door and began his preparation· by walking up and down, as his custom was, thinking out the details of the service, his sermon, the exact wording of certain phrases he wished to make.

He had been walking thus back and forth half a dozen times, when he felt the same acute pain in his side that had seized him when he fainted in church at the evening service. It passed away and he resumed his walk thinking it was only a passing disorder. But before he could turn again in his walk he felt a dizziness that whirled everything in the room about him. He clutched at a chair and was conscious of having missed it, and then he fell forward in such a way that he lay partly on the couch and partly on the floor, and became unconscious.

How long he had been in this condition he did not know, when he came to himself. He was thankful, when he did recover sufficiently to crawl to his feet and sit down on the couch, that Sarah had not seen him. He managed to get over to his desk and begin to write something as he heard her coming upstairs. He did not intend to deceive her. His thought was that he would not unnecessarily alarm her. He was very tired. It did not need much urging to persuade him to get to bed. And so, without saying anything about his second fainting attack, he went downstairs and was soon sleeping very heavily.

He awoke on Sunday morning feeling strangely calm and refreshed. The morning prayer with the

Brother . Man came like a benediction to them all.
Sarah, who had feared for Phillip, owing to the severe
strain he had been enduring, felt relieved as she saw
how he appeaied. They all prepared to go to
church, the Brother Man and William going out for
the first time since the attack on Phillip.

We have mentioned Phillip's custom of coming
into his pulpit from the little room at the side of the
platform. This morning he went in at the side door
of the church after parting with Sarah and the others.
He let Brother Man and William go on ahead a little,
and then drawing his wife to him he stooped and
kissed her. He turned at the top of the short flight
of steps leading up to the side entrance and saw her
still standing in the same place. Then she went
around from the little court to the front of the
church, and went in with the great crowd already
beginning to stream toward Calvary Church.

No one ever saw so many people in Calvary
Church before. Men sat on the platform and even
in the deep window-seats. The spaces under the
large galleries by the walls were filled mostly with
men standing there. The house was crowded long
before the hour of service. There were many beating, excited hearts in that audience. More than
one member was ashamed at the action which had
been taken, and might have wished it recalled.
With the great number of working-men and young
people in the church there was only one feeling; it
was a feeling of love for Phillip, and of sorrow for
what had been done. The fact that Phillip had

been away from the city, that he had not talked over the matter with any one, owing to his absence, the uncertainty as to how he would receive the whole thing, what he would say on this first Sunday after the letter had been written, — this attracted a certain number of persons who never go inside a church except for some extraordinary occasion, or in hopes of a sensation. So the audience that memorable day had some cruel people present, — people who narrowly watch the faces of mourners at funerals to see what ravages grief has made on the countenance.

The organist played his prelude through and was about to stop, when he saw in the glass that hung over the keys that Phillip had not yet appeared. He began again at a certain measure, repeating it, and played very slowly. By this time the church was entirely filled. There was an air of expectant waiting as the organ again ceased, and still Phillip did not come out. A great fear came over Mrs. Strong. She had half risen from her seat near the platform to go up and open the study door, when it opened and Phillip came out.

Whatever his struggle had been in that little room the closest observer could not detect any trace of tears or sorrow or shame or humiliation. He was pale, but that was common ; otherwise his face wore a firm, noble, peaceful look. As he gazed over the congregation the people felt the fascination of his glances. The first words that he spoke in the service were strong and clear. Never, had the

people seen so much to admire in his appearance
as a public speaker; and when, after the opening
exercises and the regular order of service, he rose
and came out at one side of the desk to speak, as
his custom was, the people were for the time under
the magic sway of his personality, that never stood
out so commanding and loving and true-hearted as
then.

He began to speak very quietly and simply, as his
fashion was, announcing the fact that he had been
asked to resign his pastorate of Calvary Church.
He made the statement clearly, with no halting or
hesitation or sentiment of tone or gesture. Then
after saying that there was only one course open to
him under the circumstances, he went on to speak
in defence of his interpretation of Christ and his
teaching.

" Members of Calvary Church, I call you to · bear
witness to-day; I have tried to preach to you
Christ and him crucified. I have, doubtless, made
mistakes; we all make them. I have offended
the rich men and the property-owners in Milton.
I could not help it; I was obliged to do so in order
to speak as I this moment solemnly believe my
Lord would speak. I have aroused opposition
because I asked men into the church and upon this
platform who do not call themselves Christians, for
the purpose of knowing their reasons for antagonism
to the church we love. But the time has come, O
my brothers, when the Church must welcome to its
counsels, in matters that affect the world's greatest

good, all men who have at heart the fulfilment of the Christ's teachings.

"But the cause which more than any other has led to the action of this church has been, I am fully aware, my demand that the church-members of this city should leave their possessions and go and live with the poor, wretched, sinful, hopeless people in the lower town, sharing in wise ways with them of the good things of the world. But why do I speak of all this in defence of my action or my preaching?"

Suddenly Phillip seemed to feel a revulsion of attitude toward the whole of what he had been saying. It was as if there had instantly swept over him the knowledge that he could never make the people before him understand his motive or his Christ. His speech had so far been quiet, unimpassioned, deliberate. His whole manner now underwent a swift change. People in the galleries noticed it, and men leaned out far over the gallery-railing, and more than one closed his hands tight in emotion at the sight and hearing of the tall, fiery figure on the platform.

For the intense love for the people that Phillip felt had surged into him uncontrollably. It swept away all other things. He no longer sought to justify his ways; he seemed bent on revealing to them the mighty love of Christ for them and the world. His lip trembled, his voice shook with the yearning of his soul for the people, and his frame quivered with longing.

" Yes," he said, " I love you, people of Milton beloved members of this church. I would have opened my arms to every sinful child of humanity here and shown him, if I could, the boundless love of his heavenly Father! But oh, ye would not! Ye would not! And yet the love of Christ! What a wonderful thing it is! How much he wished us to enjoy of peace and hope and fellowship and service! Yes, service, — that is what the world needs to-day; service that is willing to give all, all to Him who gave all to save us! O Christ, Master, teach us to do thy will. Make us servants to the poor and sinful and helpless. Make thy Church on earth more like thyself!"

Those nearest Phillip saw him suddenly raise his handkerchief to his lips, and then, when he took it away, it was stained with blood. But the people did not see that. And then — and then — a remarkable thing took place.

On the rear wall of Calvary Church there had been painted, when the church was built, a Latin cross. This cross had been the source of almost endless dispute among the church-members. Some said it was inartistic; others said it was in keeping with the name of the church, and had a right place in the church as part of its inner adornment. Once the dispute had grown so large and serious that the church had voted as to its removal or retention on the wall. A small majority had voted to leave it there, and there it remained. It was perfectly white, on a panel of thin wood, and stood out very conspicuous above the rear of the platform. It was not directly behind the desk, but several feet at one side.

Phillip had never made any allusion in his sermons to this feature of Calvary Church's architecture. People had wondered sometimes that with his imaginative, poetical temperament he never had done so, especially once when a sermon on the crucifixion had thrilled the people wonderfully. It might have been his extreme sensitiveness, his shrinking from anything like cheap sensation.

But now he stepped back, — it was not far, — and turning partly around, with one long arm extended toward the cross as if in imagination he saw the Christ upon it, he cried out, " ' Behold the Lamb of God that taketh away the sin of the world ! ' Yes —

> " ' In the cross of Christ I glory,
> Towering o'er the wrecks of time;
> All the light of sacred story
> Gathers round — ' "

His voice suddenly ceased, he threw his arms up, and as he turned a little forward toward the congregation he was seen to reel and stagger back against the wall. For one intense tremendous second of time he stood there with the whole church smitten into a pitying, horrified, startled, motionless crowd of blanched staring faces, as his tall dark figure towered up with outstretched arms, almost covering the very outlines of the cross, and then he sank down at its foot.

A groan went up from the audience. Several

men sprang up the platform steps. Mrs. Strong was the first person to reach the figure of her husband. Two or three helped to bear him to the front of the platform. Sarah kneeled down by him. She put her head against his breast. Then she raised her face and said calmly, " He is dead."

The Brother Man was kneeling on the other side. " No," he said with an indescribable gesture and an untranslatable inflection, " he is not dead. He is living in the eternal mansions of glory with his Lord ! "

But the news was borne from lip to lip, " He is dead ! " And that is the way men speak of the body. And they were right. The body of Phillip was dead. And the Brother Man was right also. For Phillip himself was alive in glory, and when they bore the tabernacle of his flesh out of Calvary Church that day, that was all they bore. His soul was out of the reach of humanity's selfishness and humanity's sorrow.

They said that when the funeral of Phillip Strong's body was held in Milton, rugged, unfeeling men were seen to cry like children in the streets. A great procession, largely made up of the poor and sinful, followed him to his wintry grave. They lingered long about the spot. Finally, every one withdrew except Sarah, who refused to be led away by her friends, and William and the Brother Man. They stood looking down into the grave.

" He was very young to die," at last Sarah said, with a calmness that was more terrible than bursts of grief.

"So was Christ," replied Brother Man, simply.

"But oh, Phillip, Phillip, my beloved, they killed him!" she cried; and at last, for she had not wept yet, great tears rolled down into the grave, and uncontrollable anguish seized her. Brother Man did not attempt to console or interrupt. He knew she was in the arms of God. After a long time he said: "Yes, they crucified him. But he is with his Lord now. Let us be glad for him. Let us leave him with the Eternal Peace."

.   .   .   .

When the snow had melted from the hillside and the first arbutus was beginning to bud and blossom, one day some men came out to the grave and put up a plain stone at the head. After the men had done this work they went away. One of them lingered. He was the wealthy mill-owner. He stood with his hat in his hand and his head bent down, his eyes resting on the words carved into the stone. They were these : —

PHILLIP STRONG.

Pastor of Calvary Church, Milton.

"In the cross of Christ I glory,
    Towering o'er the wrecks of time;
All the light of sacred story
    Gathers round —"

Mr. Winter looked at the incomplete line and then, as he turned away and walked slowly back down into Milton he said, "Yes, it is better so. We must complete it for him."

Ah, Phillip Strong! Thy sacrifice was not in vain! The Resurrection is not far from the Crucifixion.

.   .   .   .

Near to its close rolls up the century;
   And still the Church of Christ upon the earth
   Which marks the Christmas of his lowly birth,
Contains the selfish Scribe and Pharisee.
   O Christ of God, exchanging gain for loss,
   Would men still nail thee to the self-same cross ?

It is the Christendom of Time, and still
   Wealth and the love of it hold potent sway;
   The heart of man is stubborn to obey,
The Church has yet to do the Master's will.
   O Christ of God, we bow our souls to thee;
   Hasten the dawning of thy Church to be!

THE END.